MATED

The Wolf Pack
Book One

by
Avery Gale

Dedication

Special thanks to my cousin, David, for all his help creating the Wolf Pack's crest. I am sure there is a special place in Heaven for people with your unassuming patience.

CHAPTER ONE

"I CAN SCARCELY believe I've let you talk me into this. You must have caught me in a very weak moment is all I can fathom." Kathleen Harris was already tired of standing on the ice-coated sidewalk in four-inch stiletto black leather boots that had obviously been designed by a sadist living in a balmy climate wearing flip-flops. She and Libby really hadn't been waiting that long, but damn she hated the cold. It came as no surprise to her that people flocked to the Caribbean during their winter breaks.

"Jesus, Kit, you really need to start reading something written after the 1800s. You talk like you fell down a fucking rabbit hole into Shakespeare's living room." Libby Wells had been Kit's best friend since she'd moved to New York City twelve years ago. She was five feet nothing, but had an attitude the size of Goliath and a brilliant mind to match.

"Your lack of literary intelligence is showing, dear...wrong century by one...or two, but who's counting?" Truthfully Kit altered her speech pattern for no other reason than her own amusement most of the time. What her distracted friend didn't know was that Kit had been studying literature for nearly a century. As one of the few female werewolves in the world, she'd be almost one hundred and fifteen years old this spring. Of course in her case, age truly was just a number. As a *were* and a witch, her life expectancy was probably close to a millennium. And even though she hadn't ever actually *changed*, that was one benefit she would still get. Kit smiled to herself because considering her age and the fact her grandparents had known Shakespeare personally, Abby's comment probably wasn't too far off the mark.

God, she loved her 'grands' with everything in her and her memories of the time she spent with them always made her smile. But recently, just thinking about her parents was enough to give her indigestion. Even though they'd been nagging her for years to find her mate or mates and settle down, they'd really stepped it up the past year or two. Their relentless pressure was wearing thin...very, very thin. Hellfire, just the idea of settling down was enough to make her shudder.

Sighing to herself, she knew it wouldn't be long before she was going to be forced to move again, so hopefully she'd be out from under their watchful eyes soon enough. Her friends were already starting to comment on the fact she didn't seem to be aging, and those observations were always a sign it was getting close to time to move on. *Now that I think about it...it's actually a hell of a compliment. Considering I'm over a century, I'm doing okay.* She almost laughed out loud at her own joke. Her parents liked to remind her of her "advanced" age and her "fast approaching spinster-hood." Damn, if Libby thought Kit's language was archaic, she should meet "the parents."

If it wasn't for all the time her parents spent traveling, Kit probably would have already moved. But she really did love New York City and wasn't looking forward to having to relocate again. However, it had been a couple decades since she'd lived in New Mexico, and it was a lot warmer there...so maybe...

By the time the slow moving line brought them to the door, Kit had already started mentally organizing how she'd pack up her meager belongings. She'd discovered many, many years ago that keeping too many keepsakes was overly burdensome and owning valuable antiques tended to attract far too much attention as well. Besides, she'd have plenty of time for that when her parents passed on that monstrosity they called a summer castle. *Christ, who the hell has a fucking castle for a summer cabin? And they wonder why I don't bring my friends to visit.*

As soon as she stepped through the door of the club, Kit was nearly overwhelmed by the pounding music. As a *were*, her senses were enhanced and she couldn't imagine how music this loud would affect her if she ever *changed*. Loud music was always nearly enough to make her dizzy until she became accustomed to it. And the wall of scent she'd walked into was almost as powerful…*What is it with humans' obsession with masking their personal scents with crazy florals and musks? Jesus, most of them smell like they rolled in a flowerbed and then dipped themselves in…* Her musings were interrupted when she was hit with a scent so powerful her knees almost buckled. *Fuck, my mate. I have to get out of here before he scents me!*

Kit turned around, intent on finding Libby so she could make a quick excuse and get the frack out of the line of fire. But instead, she found herself face to chest with the owner of that intoxicating scent. *Damn, not fast enough, Kit. Make and excuse…think, damn it! Anything…just make an excuse and leave…Now!*

JAMESON WOLF HAD been almost ready to head home when

he'd taken one last look out of the front windows of his office. Looking down over the sidewalk below, he wondered why the waiting line was so long on a frigid Friday night. He'd started to turn back to the room when his eye caught on a flash of red. Damn it to hell, he'd always had a thing for auburn haired women. Redheads were rare among shifters so he took a closer look. Her long flowing mane of red curls might have been what caught his attention, but there was something about her saucy attitude that drew him in. Watching her, he saw her easy rapport with the tiny blonde beauty she was with and he liked that she seemed oblivious to the fact she turned the head of every man near her.

Making his way down the steep circular staircase he was assailed by the overpowering scents of both humans and his peers who had braved the biting cold January night in the wind swept city. He saw the red-haired beauty enter through the heavy doorway a split second before the scent of his mate barreled over him. It was as if every neuron in his brain had been suddenly struck by lightning and crackled with electrical energy. His vision tunneled and his sole mission became to find the owner of the scent and mark her as his.

As he neared the red-haired beauty who had caught his eye earlier, the exotic fragrance he'd been following became more and more potent. *Could I actually be that lucky after all these years?* Stepping up behind her, he took a deep breath letting her scent soak deeply into his soul. Even though he loved the fresh citrus smell of her hair, it was the essence of her, which nearly over-powering in its allure. It pulled him in and made every one of his senses come sharply into a pinpoint focus. He'd heard his friends describe this moment, but he had truly believed their words had been little more than romantic folly—until now.

When she turned toward him, he became instantly aware she'd been planning to escape. There was a look of panic in her eyes—what he didn't understand was what had spooked her. Awareness and anxiety were coming off her in heavy, crashing waves. He could smell fear in humans and shifters, but that wasn't what he was picking up. No, she wasn't afraid of him, but she wasn't thrilled to have been found either. *Interesting.* Mating scents are an almost overwhelmingly powerful draw for both male and female shifters so there was no doubt she had known her mate was near. So why was she trying to leave?

Both Jameson and his brother, Trevlon, were the Alphas of their pack and had been since their fathers were killed by rivals seven years ago. They had always known they'd follow pack tradition and share a mate, but they hadn't had any luck finding her, despite having traveled all over the globe searching. *How has this beauty flown under our radar? She is exactly the type of woman we are both attracted to.* "What is your name, beautiful?" Jameson knew his words had come out as more of a growl than a question, but considering how close he was to claiming her right here in the middle of the club, it was the best he could do. He relaxed a bit when he saw her deer in the headlights look. *Good. I'm happy to know she is as slammed by the attraction as I am.*

"Kit."

He heard the wobble of nervousness in her voice and could tell she had barely been able to squeak out the word so he just waited. He saw her draw in a deep breath through her mouth and almost laughed at her ineffective attempt to avoid breathing through her nose. He tried to suppress his smile when she repeated the gesture because it was a futile attempt to escape the scent of her mate.

Once a shifter found their mate, their bodies were taken over by overwhelming sexual urges that lasted for weeks. He'd seen pack members all but disappear during that time because they could barely leave their bedrooms. He waited patiently as she finally seemed to come back to awareness and answered, "I mean, Kathleen, my name is Kathleen Harris."

She was trying to look around him, which was amusing because she couldn't be more than five feet three or four inches tall and that was including the ridiculously high-heeled black leather stiletto boots she was wearing.

He was sure she hadn't meant to give him her nickname because it was likely something she reserved for those she considered close friends, so when he addressed her again, he used it deliberately. "Well, Kit, follow me, please."

He turned on his heel and started back toward the staircase when she reached out and grasped his forearm. "Wait, I can't go with you. I don't even know you. And my friend will be looking for me."

The instant she touched him he'd felt a jolt of electricity arc between them and then tiny bolts of lightning streaked up his spine. *Damn, her touch did that through the fabric of his shirt, what would it feel like when they were skin to skin?*

The twin bond between him and Trev had always been incredibly strong, so he wasn't at all surprised when his phone rang. "Where are you? Are you okay?" Typical Trevlon, straight to it—he couldn't be troubled to utter a polite greeting.

"Standing in front of a woman I want you to meet. We're in the bar, but we'll be on our way upstairs as soon as we locate her friend to let her know where we are heading. Meet us in the office in five." Jameson disconnected the call and turned to one of his staff that was walking by. He quickly gave the man a detailed description of Kit's friend and instructions to stay close to her and keep her safe until she was ready to leave the building. At that time, he was to accompany her to the office. Jameson stood six foot seven inches tall in his boots, so he could easily see the tiny blonde on the other side dance floor and directed the young man to her. Jameson was glad Charlie had been the first to walk by. He trusted the young shifter to do exactly as he'd been told.

Turning back to Kit, he realized for the first time he had taken the hand she'd used to grab his arm and was holding it in his own. He'd been rubbing small circles over the inside of her wrist with his thumb. As his gaze met hers, he felt her pulse speed up and watched as her pupils dilated. "Come along, Kit. We need to talk." This time he did smell fear so he pulled her into his arms and leaned down so his words would be painted over the soft shell of her ear like a warm brush of air, "I won't hurt you—ever. Be brave, sweet kitten."

Chapter Two

K IT FELT LIKE she'd been pushed through some kind of time warp. Suddenly everything had changed and she was now watching her life play out from the outside looking in. Some kind of damn fog seemed to have settled over her brain and she found herself passively following the man who had approached her at the bar like some love-struck fool. He was her mate and that was the last thing she'd been looking for when she left home tonight. He was pulling her through the crowd, heading toward a tall spiral staircase. *Oh hell no. I don't fucking think so.*

She dug in her heels despite the fact she nearly had her arm jerked out of its socket for her trouble. "Excuse me, but I'm not leaving here with you. I don't even know your name. Hell's bells and hand grenades...you could be Jack the Ripper's long lost sixth cousin for all I know." Damn it to hell. He had just smiled at her, and then turned and started pulling her after him again. "Hey, I said I wasn't going with you. Is your brain addled or are you simply ignoring me? What is your name anyway? And by what authority did you get that man to agree to take care of Libby? And just exactly what does that entail anyway?"

She saw his shoulders shaking. If he was laughing at her, she was going to go bat-shit on him before he made it to his beloved office. When she tried to wrench her hand from his, he simply tightened his grip. As they neared a spiral stairway, she started to panic and her brain seemed finally to click fully back into gear. Damn it, how had this happened? She'd managed to avoid finding her mate all these years only to be blindsided during a simple club-hop. *I swear if anyone tells my parents about this, I'll shred them limb from bony limb.*

When they reached the top of the stairs, she was relieved to find the music was much more muted and the small tables were filled with people engaged in much more intimate behavior than she'd seen downstairs. She also noticed every table had one woman and multiple men. She smelled the distinct scents of other shifters and knew immediately she was seeing mated couples. And she used the term *couples* loosely, because these were not pairs but ménages and more. Both of her parents were shifters, but Kit hadn't been raised in a pack, so her knowledge of the workings of their social order was greatly limited. She did know it was common for mated groups to involve more than one male, particularly when the males are siblings. Damn, she didn't even want *one* mate, let alone two…or more. *Frack!*

When she tried yet again to pry her hand from his, he finally stopped and turned toward her. "Kit, I have already told you I won't hurt you, but we need to talk so behave." Then, as if he needed to soften his command, he brought his free hand up to her face and drew his fingertips slowly from her temple down her jawline and then cupped her jaw so her face was tilted up to his. "Let's see if this helps," and then he leaned down and sealed his lips over hers. The flavor of him burst over her pallet in an explosion of raw desire so potent it was as if her taste buds had suddenly came awake after a lifetime of being comatose. She immediately felt her sex flood with moisture in response and the silk thong she was wearing was soaked within seconds. She worried the evidence of her arousal would be trailing down the insides of her thighs if he continued his oral seduction. His tongue was dancing inside her mouth and she found herself pushing closer so her ample cleavage was pressed intimately against his chest. He literally growled when he finally backed away from the kiss. Realizing the kiss had ended, she slowly opened her eyes and found she was almost dizzy. She wasn't sure if she was lightheaded from a lack of oxygen or from the potency of the man who had been kissing her, but she realized she was almost panting as she struggled to regain her focus.

She finally found her voice, "No. I don't want this. I don't want to be mated. Please, let me go." She was sure the airy words weren't going to be very credible, but she felt better for having tried.

He'd moved his mouth back to her ear and licked the outer shell before whispering, "Oh my sweet kitten, I can smell your arousal so your denial falls on deaf ears. And that lovely short skirt you are wearing means I can slide my fingers all the way into your wet heat to find out if you are wet for me. And I'd love to feel my fingers sliding through your honey, but I have someone I would like for you to meet first. But, kitten, the choice is yours. We can continue to my office to meet my brother or I can finger fuck you into oblivion right here in front of several of our pack members who are already watching us with avid interest. What's it going to be, Kit?"

She swayed on her feet, but managed to recover enough to brace herself before her knees folded. She was worried she might have an orgasm from his words alone and the feel of his warm breath pushing desire over her ear and into her mind was chipping away at her resistance. His voice was pure sex set to sound and she shuddered at how effective it was. Having an audience was not the way she wanted this discussion to go down, so she opted to continue to his office. "Office" was all she managed to squeeze past the lump in her throat, but it must have been enough because he quickly resumed his long strides down a hall she hadn't even noticed they were standing near when she'd pulled him to a stop.

TREVLON WOLF HAD scented their mate before his brother had even walked through the door of their office with her. His first look at her stole his breath. Every man, whether or not a shifter, dreams his mate will be beautiful. But he'd never dared to imagine he and Jameson would be lucky enough to get a mate as drop-fucking-dead gorgeous. And he could smell her arousal, and it was an intoxicating blend of temptation and pure sexual fantasy. He stepped forward as they came further into the large room. "Introduce me, brother." He knew his words sounded harsh, but he wasn't going to waste a single moment. He wanted her naked and spread out in front of him ten minutes ago.

"Kit, this is my baby brother, Trevlon. Trev, this is Kathleen Harris." Trevlon didn't miss the fact she was staring at him. As identical twins, he and Jameson were well accustomed to this reaction.

"Baby brother? Aren't you twins? I mean, how can you not be twins?"

Trev watched as her eyes went wide and her nostrils flared. He would have bet his last nickel she'd suddenly concluded she was mated to them both.

"Oh, crap on a cactus. Tell me you don't think you are

both my mates. Hell, I don't want or need one mate, let alone two."

He nearly laughed out loud when her eyes went wide with alarm.

"Shit, there aren't any more of you are there? Like those groups out at those tables…each table only had one women and two or more men. Damn, I'm going to kick Libby's ass, this is all her fault. And if she tells my parents I'll have to kill her, I don't want to, but I will. And she'll have it coming, too. Fuck me. This is a disaster of Biblical proportions."

Trev had been enjoying her little tirade. Personally he could see a lot of benefits to having their woman ramble. Obviously she was thinking out loud and that would certainly work to their benefit. Glancing toward his brother, he was sure Jameson was thinking the same thing because he recognized the sly smile. Deciding to just reach out and take her small hand in his to see what effect it had, he was shocked, literally, at the surge of electrical energy he felt race up his arm. He smiled when he saw her expressive eyes go wide in surprise. *Oh yeah, baby, you felt it too didn't you?*

Trev led Kit to a sofa facing the fireplace and pulled her down beside him. "Baby, there is no use denying what we all know is true, and that is we are mates. And no, it is just my *older* brother and I. And by the way, you are right, we are identical twins and he is three minutes older." Trev was still holding her hand and he was pleased that she hadn't pulled her tiny hand from his. Looking into her emerald eyes, he saw a wariness that made him wonder who had hurt her. When he took a deep breath, the smell of her arousal filled his body and ignited a hunger he wasn't going to be able to tamp down much longer.

"Jameson, update me." Trev wanted to know what his brother had told her about them. Jameson had moved so he was sitting on the other side of Kit and was leaning in close to her. Trev saw the raw hunger that was ravaging him reflected in his brother's face and knew Jameson was probably as desperate to sink into her, as he was himself.

"I hadn't even told her my name, so she has no idea who we are. From her reaction to the starlight room, I'm guessing that even though she is a shifter she knows little about the social workings or politics of packs. She's made it very clear she doesn't want to be mated, so it's the first thing we'll need to discuss." Jameson was uncharacteristically snide and Trev wondered why. When he looked at his brother and simply raised a brow, Jameson merely shrugged. "I don't understand why she's fighting this. It's not like we're the worst catches on the planet."

And there it was—the crux of the matter was that Jameson Wolf wasn't used to being rejected. Trev was sure their beautiful mate could be persuaded, but first they'd need to find out what her objection was based on. Turning to Kit, he smiled and then using his finger, he turned her chin so she was facing him. "Kit, we'll explain everything as we go along, but first I want you to answer a question. And I want you to answer it with complete honesty. Can you do that for me?"

He watched and waited as she seemed to weigh her options, when she finally nodded her head he smiled and leaned forward to kiss the tip of her nose. "Good enough. Now, why are you so desperately afraid of being mated?"

Chapter Three

K IT WAS REELING and each time she thought she was close to getting her feet under her again, she was hit with another wave of soul-altering arousal. Trevlon Wolf's sweet kiss on the end her nose had pushed his scent deep inside her and it had wrapped its tentacles in a deep spiral all the way to her soaking sex. The entire time she had been sitting in their office she'd been trying to figure out why she didn't just leave and she still hadn't come up with a plausible answer.

The room itself was spectacular. Polished wood floors and intricately carved moldings gave the setting a distinctive Victorian look. But it was the enormous fireplace made of shiny black onyx that was the focal point of the room. Having a mother who was a witch had its advantages and she was well versed in the magical powers of onyx. The look of the entire office spoke volumes that all led to one undeniable conclusion, this room was the home territory of raw male power and had been influenced by magic, whether or not they knew it. A mantle made from a glistening slab of gray granite topped off the fireplace and the mirror that hung above the mantle was slanted so it reflected the entire room. The large window to her left featured an interesting symbol consisting of a triangle with a night forest scene, a howling wolf, and a wolf print. It was a spectacular piece of glass and none of the symbolism was lost on her. Even with her limited knowledge of pack life, she recognized what her father had told her was the "call to power" of the were packs that fought for good.

Moving her gaze around the room, she noticed each piece of furniture in the room was over-sized, no doubt owing to the very tall men who did their business here. Oddly there didn't seem to be much paperwork on the desks and Kit wondered briefly if they actually worked here or if it was more of a fancy place to meet people. *Oh shit. It's probably the place they bring women they want to... Eww, so not going there.*

She finally came back from her musings and realized they were both looking at her expectantly. *Damn it, Kit, pay attention. Shit, what did he ask? Fear? Did he say something about fear?* "I'm sorry, could you repeat the question please? I'm afraid I got lost in thought for a few seconds there."

She heard Jameson's snort from beside her, "A few seconds my ass. Where did you go anyway?"

Trev looked at Jameson and shook his head. "Baby, never mind him, he has never been the most patient person around and the burden of his responsibilities as our pack's Alpha doesn't tend to do much to help the situation." Kit knew the leaders of shifter packs carried a huge burden on their shoulders, but she didn't understand why he'd have to do it alone if they were twins. The only thing she could come up with was that since he was the oldest he was forced to carry the majority of the burden.

Trevlon smiled at her and said, "We'll ask you more about these little mental road trips you take some another time. Right now, I'm more interested in finding out why you are so opposed to being mated. And specifically I'd like to know why you are opposed to being mated with us."

Concentrate, Kit. Damn, you have to get your shit together and get out of here. They know exactly how to play this game and you are fucking clueless. You have just walked into a battle with a butter knife. And there are two of them and they are gorgeous and smell amazing and...damn it focus. "Well, I have been thinking about moving and I don't want to be stuck here. You know how it is. Can't stay anywhere too long, because, well...people start to notice when you don't age." She kept her eyes lowered because she was worried they'd see straight through her lie. She had never been very good at deception because for the most part, she simply had never cared enough to even practice. Her feeling had always been, if you don't like me, feel free to move along, because the door that let you *in* will also let you *out.* Having lived as long as she had, she knew relationships with humans tended to be very transient, so it had always been easier to just move on.

Kit didn't have any intention of telling either of them that she was the product of a very unusual mating. Nor did she plan to explain that becoming mated herself was the very thing that would set her magical powers free. Kit's mother was a very powerful witch whose true powers hadn't been realized until she had mated with Kit's father.

Kit had always known she would come into her magical powers when she mated and she had every intention of continuing to avoid it like the plague, thank you very much. Hell, even she knew that with immense magical ability came crushing responsibility. And quite frankly, she was having too much fun to be forced to spend her time fighting the battles she knew her mother and grandmother traveled the world to face.

"Baby, tell us what you know about being a mated shifter. And what does it mean to you specifically?" Trev Wolf's voice was like the smoothest whiskey and likely just as addictive. She was trying to force herself to concentrate on the words themselves and not fall into the seductive cadence of his voice, but there was a hypnotic quality to it that drew her in and held her as if she'd been tied down. Oh and that was a mental picture she certainly hadn't needed. Being bound and spread wide for their pleasure was exactly where she longed to be, but she needed to stop letting her hormones lead her thoughts.

She'd never had an orgasm that was brought on by anything that didn't require batteries, but she instinctively recognized the telltale flutters in her clit. Shifting in her seat and crossing her legs, she hoped to stop the evidence of her arousal from soaking into the cushion under her. She had to suppress a shudder, holy crap, just thinking about that was mortifying. But Jameson reached over and pulled her leg back down and then spread them further apart. "Oh no you don't, kitten. You are trying to hide your arousal from us and we won't allow it. And it wouldn't matter, because we'd be able to smell your sweet pussy for several miles if conditions were ideal, and if we're in the same room with you, there is absolutely no way you can mask it. After we've claimed you, we'll be able to tell you things about your body that you probably can't yet even imagine." He'd been rubbing gently up and down the inside of her thigh and the movement drew her with its almost magnetic force despite her best efforts to fight it. The battle was really with herself, since falling under his spell was inevitable. When Trev gently tugged her other leg she felt a white-hot streak of need pulse from her clit to her core. She moaned and felt her legs fall open.

There was a small part of her brain that kept fighting to surface, and it was trying to warn her about something, but the voice was being drowned out by the sound of blood rushing through her ears. No doubt the blood coursing past her ears was heading south to join all the rest. And all of the pooling was making her pussy feel like it was swelling and throbbing in time with her rapidly beating heart. She could feel Trev leaning close, and when he drew his tongue up the side of her neck, pausing to press it flat against the pulse point, she arched her back and cried out, "Oh, God, please."

"Please what, baby? I can't give you what you want until I know what it is." She knew he was playing her, but she was so swamped with the pure animalistic desire that was clawing its way to the surface she couldn't manage to care.

"Please touch me," Kit barely recognized her own voice but at that moment, she didn't care how needy she sounded. Goddess help her, she was going to implode if one of them didn't touch her pussy soon.

"Oh, baby, it's going to be our pleasure to touch you. Lean back against Jameson." She felt them shift her so her back was against Jameson's massive chest and his hands slid under her shirt to cup her breasts over the barely there lace bra she'd worn. When he gently pinched her nipples, she felt them stiffen and peak to even sharper points than they were already. The slight zing of pain had just made her pussy wetter and she realized she was arching and pressing closer into his touch. For several minutes she just leaned against him and lost herself in the feeling of his warm, calloused fingers through her bra. Finally she heard his growl as he easily ripped the fabric of her shirt and bra so he could bare her breasts to his touch in one swift motion.

"Open your eyes, baby. I want you to see how much I want you." She had to force her eyes open and was grateful she had because the look on Trevlon Wolf's face was one she would remember until the end of time. His beautiful features were tight, his focus and lust for her was written in each line and curve of his face. But it was the blatant desire that stole her breath. Kit felt like her skin was tingling and she worried briefly if the feeling wasn't some prelude to a release of magical power. What if her mother and grandmother had been wrong? What if all it took to release her power was an orgasm at the hand of one of the mates the fates had chosen for her?

Suddenly Kit felt herself panting for breath and not from her arousal, oh no, this was pure unmitigated panic. Trev must have sensed the shift in her because his eyes searched hers and he scooted up so his face was directly in front of hers. "Baby, take a deep breath. No, slow it down. Stop. Now I want you to focus, Kit." Kit was trying to follow his instructions, but she felt like she was a caught inside a snowball that someone had casually pushed over the top of a mountain. It was a steep fall and she was gaining speed.

She felt Jameson pull her up on to his lap and then his commanding tone flooded her awareness, "Focus on our voices, kitten. Let the words seep deeply into your fear so it shatters. I don't know what sent you into this storm, but we're here to pull you back. We'll always be here. That is something you need to know about us, love. And there is nothing the three of us can't face together."

Kit locked on to his face as well as his words as if they were lifelines. But even though she appreciated his confidence, she knew they wouldn't want anything to do with her once they knew what destiny held for her if she let herself become their mate. And honestly, who could blame them? She'd seen the torment her father went through being married to her mother. The weeks and months her mom spent away from home fighting the darkest forces the underworld had to offer, those that were so powerful they continually threatened the delicate balance between the light and dark of the world.

There wasn't any doubt she was wildly attracted to these men, but it wasn't them she feared. No, her real fear was she didn't want to give up the life she had enjoyed for so many years. She wasn't ready to spend all of her time devoted to fighting a battle that would never be truly won. But she wondered if maybe...just maybe she could give herself over to the pleasures they could provide and not actually become *mated*. As she understood it, they had to actually claim her in order for her magic to be released. So the real question was actually whether or not it was fair to them to enjoy the unbridled pleasure she was sure they could give her and then simply walk away? She could easily disappear again, so hell yes, the pleasure was sounding more and more possible. And then she'd move on—no one would look for her in New Mexico.

When Kit had finally decided the chance to give her body over to the pleasure, even if it could only be once, she knew these two men would make certain it had been worth it. She'd always wondered how good sex with the right partner might be and from the way she been feeling a few minutes ago, it was going to be spectacular.

Kit took a deep breath and then smiled, "I'm sorry, I was just a bit overwhelmed for a bit. I'm okay now." And then leaning forward, she pulled Jameson's lips to hers and put everything she had into a kiss she hoped would take them right back where they had been a few minutes ago.

Chapter Four

J AMESON HAD BEEN lost in his efforts to track Kit's mutterings when she had leaned forward and slammed him
with a scorching lip-lock. For the first time in years he had
been totally surprised by a woman. Had he really heard her
right? Did she say something about getting her magical
powers if she mated? He had been afraid to chance looking
at Trev while she'd been murmuring all that craziness to
see if his brother was as lost as he was. The one thing Kit
had said that had shocked him to his core was about
running to New Mexico and something about her mother
and grandmother traveling the world to fight the darkness.

Try as he might to puzzle it out, Jameson wasn't able
to think about anything but the softness of Kit pressing her
tightly peaked and gloriously bare nipples against his chest
and the feel of her hungry mouth exploring his like she was
starving for him. He had let her control things long
enough, it was time to take the reins back in hand. Sliding
his hands into the silky strands of her hair, he wrapped his
fingers in the red waves and pulled back so she knew he
was now controlling the pace. He knew the exact moment
she registered the change by the smell of her renewed
arousal flooding his senses. *Seems our mate responds well to
the power exchange.*

Jameson and Trevlon had shared a lot of women over
the years so their ability to read each other's movements

was well tuned. James gave Trev a quick hand signal and felt him immediately begin removing the rest of Kit's clothing. Honestly, if he didn't sink his aching cock inside her quickly, he was going to come in his pants like an inexperienced teenager, and that was *not* how he wanted this to go down.

"Kitten, Trev and I want to feel every inch of you. And we fully intend to fuck you. Are you ready for us? Are you aching for our cocks as much as we're aching to feel your slick heat wrapping itself around us? We're going to make this so good you'll crave it again and again. As much as I'd love to have our first time be in some exquisitely romantic location, the simple fact is I can't wait, I want you too much." The words he'd spoken couldn't have been truer, and his mind was already beginning to fog from the raging current of his desire for her.

He felt Kit arch her back and watched as Trev made the most of her movement by pulling the remnants of her shirt and bra down her toned arms. Trev leaned close to her and Jameson heard his words and had to smile at his clever manipulation. "Show us that you want us as much as we want you—help me take off this skirt, baby." Jameson knew Trev's words served two purposes, first, they gave her a chance to show her consent through her compliance and secondly, they got her naked a whole lot quicker. *Clever bastard, my brother.*

Jameson heard her quick intake of breath at Trev's words and wondered for just a moment if she was going to refuse. But she finally pulled her lips from his and slowly stood in front of them. Watching her, he was sure he would remember this moment for the rest of his life. The way she looked as she stood in front of them with the soft orange glow of the fire shining around her as a backlight.

The tumble of her mussed hair as it framed her beautiful face like a halo of glowing rubies strung together with ribbons of red and gold. There was gentleness in her expression in direct contract to the wanton smile on her lips that were swollen from their kisses. But it was the look of pure, raw desire that lit her eyes that he knew would be the focal point of his memory of this moment.

"Kitten, you take my breath away." Jameson reached forward, slid his fingers through her silky folds, and was thrilled to find her soaking wet. "Your body shows its desire for your mates, my love." He felt her stiffen for just a second before the feel of his fingers pulled her right back into the mist of lust. "That's a good girl. Let us make you feel good. I promise you this is going to rock your world sweetness."

Jameson and Trev had always been able to communicate telepathically better than most unmated shifters because of their twin bond so he wasn't surprised to hear Trev's question, *'Slide a finger in her, is she tight?'* Shifters were able to communicate telepathically by necessity, but the strength of that link and the ability to focus in on one person or one group at the exclusion of others had always depended on the shifter's mating status and whether or not they were the pack's Alphas. Jameson remembered their fathers talking about how quickly they had been able to mind-speak with their mother. Their dads had claimed the enhanced ability had started even before they'd claimed her as their mate and had resulted from the fact their mate had also been a witch.

Moving his fingers closer to her opening, Jameson watched as Trev stood and moved behind her. His brother had removed his shirt so when he pulled her back against his chest Jameson saw her eyes glaze over at the feeling of

Trev's chest hair against her bare back. Sliding his middle finger just inside her wet heat, Jameson froze.

'Holy fucking hell—she's a virgin. Christ I don't know whether to praise the Gods or shut this down until we can find out more.' Jameson glanced up and saw the concern in Trev's expression a split second before he noticed what he recognized as embarrassment and humiliation that now filled Kit's eyes. Jameson knew in that moment if they hesitated, she'd see it as a rejection and run at the first opportunity. Then they'd spend months, maybe years, searching for her. *Not happening, my sweet mate. We've already waited much too long for you.*

"Kitten, you know this doesn't change our desire for you, right? I can tell by your eyes you think differently, but I assure you this is the greatest gift you could have ever given us." He leaned forward, pressed a kiss to her naval, and was pleased to feel her channel flood his fingers with another wave of honey. "The only thing that changes is the tempo. We'll make sure you are as prepared as you can be before I push through and claim the treasure you have guarded and saved just for us."

Jameson felt her relax, but just fractionally. Unfortunately the break in the arousal would have to be rebuilt quickly, it was likely she would over-think the situation. And he was sure that given too much time to reconsider, she would likely decide it was time to retreat. And the bottom line was, the choice to mate was always the female's to make. Oh sure, they could and would try to persuade her, but ultimately the choice would be hers.

He continued moving his fingers in slow strokes from her clit to her tight rear hole and noticed how her eyes darkened with each pass. Varying the intensity of his touch just enough to keep her on edge, he found himself lost in the feel of her warm syrup coating his fingers. Something about her earlier mutterings was still lingering in the back of his mind and tickling at his awareness, but he knew he had to let it go so he could concentrate on the woman who was quickly making him insane with the need to be inside her and then claim her as his own. The smell of her arousal was heady and her body was so primed he was sure he could make her come with a simple command if she'd just allow herself to be led with her body rather than her head.

Jameson knew commanding her to orgasm required a level of trust they had yet to build but that didn't stop him from fantasizing about it. "Kitten, your body is speaking for you. Let us show you how wonderful sex can be when your pleasure is the focus of your two mates. We'll take you to the mountain peak and then let you sail on the winds of your release."

Trev leaned over her shoulder and spoke against her ear, "Baby, everything about you makes me crazy with need. I can barely contain my desire to feel your pussy squeezing my cock as I slide in and out of you. Jameson and I will push you, never doubt that. But we'll never hurt you and the ultimate control is always yours." Jameson watched as his brother's arm banded around her torso so her breasts were lifted even further and appeared to be an offering from Mother Nature herself. "Your breasts are amazing and I can't wait to pull your pink nipples into my mouth and press them against the roof of my mouth. You'll arch into the touch because it will be electrifying. Let's step back so Jameson can get undressed and you'll see just how much he wants you."

Jameson was pleased to see she was once again sliding down the slippery slope of unabated arousal. Trev held her tightly against his chest and let her watch as Jameson quickly stripped out of his clothes. He nearly moaned when his engorged cock was finally freed from his tight leather pants. When he looked up and saw her eyes go wide, he leaned forward and kissed her forehead. "Don't worry, kitten. It will fit just fine, you'll see." Then kneeling in front of her he didn't waste any time setting his mouth to her.

Using his tongue to probe her slick channel, Jameson nearly lost his mind at the taste of her. With her scent surrounding him, he scooped the sweet honey from her vagina with his tongue and moaned as it coated his throat. When he felt her start to shudder, he focused his attention on her clit. Circling the tiny nerve bundle in tighter and tighter spirals, working it until it was pulsing against his tongue. When he bit down on it gently, Kit detonated in a screaming release that sent spurts of her sweet cream over his tongue. Jameson continued lapping at her until he felt the final shudders of her release fade away. Leaning back he looked up and saw Trev's smile as he heard his brother speak in his mind. *'I've got her, get things set up and we'll make her ours.'*

Jameson nodded quickly then set to work, because he couldn't wait to slide in to her for the first time. He moved to the mantel and picked up the small remote and with the press of a button, the wall along the right side of the fireplace rolled quietly into the hidden pocket in the wall and revealed the bedroom few knew existed. He smiled at her gasp when Trev leaned down and scooped her up in his arms and headed through the door.

Jameson took the time to hit the locks on their office door and start the stereo system before making his way to her side. As the strains of "Bella's Lullaby" by Carter Burwell filled the air, the significance of a love song from the *Twilight* soundtrack wasn't lost on him. Trev held her while Jameson pulled down the bedspread and arranged the pillows. He watched his brother lay Kit gently on the bed before removing his pants. Jameson smiled when he saw how his brother's eyes never left their emerald colored windows to Kit's soul. She was almost panting with need by the time they flanked her again. It was a tradition in their pack that the oldest was the first to fuck their mate, so Jameson positioned himself between her ivory thighs and moved the tip of his rigid length through her wet silk. "Oh, kitten, your pussy is so wet and hot. The slick, hot silk tempts me in ways I've never experienced. I'm going to go as slow as I can."

Using his knees to spread her legs even wider, he leaned over her and held most of his weight on his bent arms, but he wanted her to feel a small portion of his weight to know that he was surrounding her. It wasn't about holding her down—it was about wrapping her senses in him. He wanted to imprint the scent of his skin into her subconscious mind so when she dreamed, it would be of him. Jameson also wanted her to experience his weight pressing against her breasts as she took in the look of desire he knew was reflected in his eyes. But most of all he wanted her to hear his words of encouragement and know she could feel each breath he took as he slid so deeply inside her she wouldn't be able to tell where she ended and he began.

Letting his hunger spill over into his words, he whispered against her ear, "Kitten, I'm going to begin slowly, but there will come a point when I will just have to push through. Don't hide the pain from us. It belongs to Trev and to me. We'll make it a fleeting memory but we have to get you past it first." He'd been rocking his hips gently sliding through the wet folds and then just barely letting the tip of his cock open her pussy to his exploration. Suddenly she shifted her hips and bucked up so he slid in far enough that he pushed through the thin membrane. Just as she screamed his name he felt a tear roll down her cheek. "Oh fuck. Kitten, please hold still. Christ, I can't believe you did that. Oh, pet, it could have been so much easier for you if you had—oh, Kit, for fuck's sake hold still." She had wrapped her arms around his back and was trying desperately to arch again so his cock would slide deeper. She was testing his control seven ways to Sunday and he was about a split second from giving her the pounding she was seeking. *'God damn it, Trev, do something. Hold on to her or I'm going to fuck her into the mattress and that isn't how this should go.'* Jameson was grateful for their telepathic link because he wasn't sure he would have had enough control to actually speak the words. And God almighty, he wasn't going to be able to hold off much longer with her writhing and bucking under him. When Trev locked his hands around her wrists and held them over her head it seemed to settle her enough that Jameson was able to catch his breath.

"Oh please, I need you to move. Oh, Jameson, don't stop, please." Her words were all it took for his control to snap. Jameson started stroking in and out of her slick channel, gaining depth with each move. "Oh my God, that feels so good. I can feel each ridge as you move inside me. It's an electric need...that I can't stop..." Jameson felt her pussy clamp down on him like a vice and even though he wasn't all the way in yet, his own release erupted from him like a volcano. Just as she seemed to reach the peak of her release, her skin started to sparkle. He attributed it to the candlelight reflecting in the perspiration beading on her face and chest, but it was still an amazing sight.

"Mine." Jameson could barely breathe and as he struggled to hold himself up so she wasn't crushed beneath his weight, he realized how shocked he'd been by his own release. He had planned to pull out since they hadn't discussed birth control, but there hadn't been time. Or perhaps he had chosen to ignore that moment when he should have *taken time.* Despite knowing what he should have done, he couldn't suppress the primal part of him that was satisfied beyond measure when he felt his seed flow from her as he pulled out of her delicious body.

Taking the warm cloth Trev handed him, he gently cleaned his cum from her and grimaced at the amount of blood he saw. He sealed her lips in a scorching kiss before he told her how proud he was of her before moving aside so Trev could experience the joy of making love to her as well.

CHAPTER FIVE

TREVLON WOLF DIDN'T claim to know everything about women, but he knew this much—the one lying on the bed in front of him would gather her defenses in a heartbeat if he gave her a chance. As soon as Jameson stepped back from Kit, Trev laid down alongside her. Softly tracing ancient rune symbols of protection over her heart and belly, he just watched as she let her desire bubble up yet again.

The symbols were reinforced by his words as he recited the chants he'd heard the night his parents had been killed as he and Jameson had fought to get to them. Their mother had locked them out when another Wiccan shifter had shown up to help. But in the end the two women hadn't been able to hold off all the darkness that had surrounded them. His parents had all died and the woman who had risked her life to help them had been seriously hurt. They hadn't even gotten to see her because she'd been whisked away before they'd been able to get past the shields their mother had been put in place.

Speaking telepathically to Jameson, Trev asked, *'Do you think it was her mother?'* At Jameson's confused look, he added, *'The witch who tried to help Mom and the Dads?'* He watched as his twin's eyes went wide.

'Fuck! I knew there was something about her words that un-settled me, but I couldn't figure it out. Hell, her skin really did

emit tiny bits of light when she came, didn't it? We'll need to find out. If so, none of this is an accident. But right now, you need to bind her to you through pleasure until we can claim her.'

Trev agreed and quickly refocused every bit of his attention on the amazing woman spread out before him. Lowering his lips to the peaks of her pink nipples, he circled the areola of each breast with the very tip of his tongue and then blew a soft puff of air over each one and watched them draw up tightly. "I can't wait to see these decorated with beautiful diamonds dangling from a delicate golden chain. What is your birthstone, baby?"

"Sapphire," her voice was already becoming airy and infused with desire just as Trev had hoped it would.

"Oh, baby girl, you'll look lovely in that color. I can already see the short silk dress hugging your body as we walk you to one of the private booths downstairs for dinner. You'll wear the dress we've given you, but nothing else. Your bare pussy exposed for our pleasure. As we enjoy our dinner, we'll have you between us and your legs spread wide so our fingers are dancing through your wet folds. The music will hide the sounds your wet pussy will make as our fingers fuck you to the very edge of release over and over. But we won't let you come until we give you permission. You'll be wild with a blazing need that bubbles up from the depths of your soul. You'll be begging us to fuck you with our cocks right there no matter who might see you. The fact you have an audience won't matter before we're through."

One of the wonderful things about being a shifter was the ability to hear a woman's soft sighs and whimpers of need as well as the rushing blood as their bodies flooded their sex organs in preparation for the cocks of their mates. Trev could hear Kit's heart pounding as she processed his words and the smell of her arousal was now overriding the smell of the blood she'd lost a few minutes ago. When he'd smelled her blood and known she'd been in pain, he'd almost lost his mind.

"I'm going to fuck you, baby. Roll over and get up on your hands and knees." When she didn't move immediately, he let a bit of steel infuse his words. "Now, Kit. Don't make me give you a spanking." He knew his words had been risky, but he was rewarded by her soft intake of breath and quick scramble to comply. When he ran his fingers through the soaking wet lips of her pussy, he smiled. "Oh, sweetness, you are so wet for me. Maybe a spanking on your lovely bare ass isn't much of a punishment threat after all. We'll have to explore that one day soon, but first I want you to lower yourself down on to your forearms. That's perfect. Now, close your eyes and let me in. Listen to my words for as long as your mind will let you hold on. But don't come until I tell you that you can. Do you understand?"

Her voice was muffled by the tangle of sheets but he heard her say "I'll try" just as he pushed deeply into her. Her gasp and her automatic tightening around him told him all he needed to know. He set a steady rhythm stroking deeply but never fast enough to send her over. "Oh, please. I need more. Please, just a little more." He loved the sound of her sweet begging and could barely keep from giving her exactly what she was asking for.

"Please what, baby? Tell me what you want more of and maybe I can help you find it," his words were hoarse because he was using so much of his energy to keep from going off like a rocket on the fourth of July. He looked down at her ivory skin, dewy from her arousal and marveled at how smooth and perfect it looked spread before him in a nearly perfect submissive posture. Their mate was flawless and he felt himself getting closer and closer to the point of no return. Pushing in just a bit, he was already fighting to maintain his control as her heat began pulling him deeper and deeper inside. It was almost as if his body was proceeding without his consent.

"Oh, Trev, I need to feel your cock moving inside me. It feels so very good and I can barely think because my mind is awash in all the sensations. It feels like there is fire shooting up and down my spine." He watched as she arched her back and tried to push back against him to impale herself on his cock.

"Hold still, Kit. If you try to take me too soon I'm going to paddle your ass. We don't want you to be too sore or we won't be able to do this again and again. And your pussy is lighting me up, baby. I am barely holding on here. You don't want to challenge me on this, trust me. I want nothing more than to pound you in to the mattress, to lean over and sink my teeth in to your shoulder and make you mine. I'm skating on a very fine edge, baby, so don't push me."

Trev continued to hold Kit's hips tightly as he slowly rocked into her hot cunt. She was still squeezing his cock each time he pulled back and she'd stopped trying to shove back. But the mewing sounds of need she was making were threatening to make him lose his last shred of sanity. And when he felt her shift herself lower and then felt her soft hand wrap around his balls and give them a light squeeze it was all over. "Oh fuck, baby, that feels so good. Jameson, move Kit's hands over her head and kept them there. She has just stolen the last of my control and this is going to be over much too soon and I want to take her with me."

He saw his brother pull their mate's hands over her

head and that shift in position was enough that his cock was now grazing her G-spot with each stroke and Trev barely managed to get out, "Come for me, Kit" before she was screaming her release. Feeling her tight passage flood with cream was all it took to send him over the edge with her. There was no better feeling in the world than knowing he'd just marked his mate with his seed. The only thing more satisfying would be claiming her with his bite. Trev knew she wasn't in heat because both he and Jameson would be able to smell that immediately. But knowing he'd left a part of himself deep inside her fanned a spark of his inner wolf and it was something he'd never experienced with another woman. *Mine!*

It was taking him a long time to regain his ability to form coherent words even though he was trying. When his brain and mouth finally decided to work together, he spoke quietly to her, "Baby, I really have no words to describe how amazing that was. You just stole a large part of my soul—please take good care of it, because it's yours to hold forever." He knew it would only take him a few minutes to recover and then he'd be swimming in his desire to take her again so he leaned back so Jameson could once again distract her.

Trev watched as Jameson leaned down and kissed Kit with a desperate hunger, it was obvious he was mired in the same heavy emotion of the moment that Trev was trying to wade through. Trev listened to Jameson speak in the compelling voice that only a pack's Alpha was accustomed to using. "Kit, come home with us. Spend the next week at our home. Give us a chance to show you how great a life with us could be. If you still want to leave at the end of a week, we'll let you walk away. We won't like it— but we'll keep our word. You owe it to yourself and to us to give this a chance, particularly since you aren't that familiar with the ways of a pack. It would also give you a chance to explore what seems to be a largely unfamiliar part of your heritage."

Trev had to bite his tongue to keep from screaming the words pounding through his head. *'I don't fucking think so. There is no way we're walking away from her. God dammit to hell, she belongs to us and we'll never let her go.'* He didn't miss the glimmer of recognition in Jameson's eyes, so Trev knew his twin had picked up on the denial racing through Trev's thoughts.

There was no doubt that Jameson Wolf could be a conniving bastard and had been known to use every available resource when it came to what was best for their pack. Trev hoped like hell his twin had some sort of a plan, so he tried desperately to hold back his protests—at least for the moment. Turning to his side he leaned up, propped his head on his hand, and watched as emotions raced through her deep green eyes. He knew she was still feeling the effects of the endorphins that had flooded her from the two powerful orgasms and likely that was exactly as his brother had planned it. Trev could feel Jameson's emotions and knew his brother was counting on those little chemical jewels to tip the scales in their favor.

Trev could see she was nervous about going home with two men she didn't know aside from having them fuck her into the mattress. He also knew she was probably also desperately trying to reign in her olfactory system as it screamed at her to let them mate her. "Baby, how about if you invite your friend to join us for the weekend. It's a big house and there are always plenty of people around. We'll make sure she is returned to the city Sunday evening so she can be at work on Monday."

"But, I don't have anything with me...I mean, who packs for a week when they are just planning to go to a club for a bit of dancing?" Trev knew her brain was starting to come back on-line and that wasn't going to help their cause at all. "And I don't know if taking Libby is a good idea, I mean she doesn't know anything about me being a shifter and a—" Trev watched as her eyes went wide as she caught herself.

Evidently Jameson was going to let her "near-slip" go for now because he simply leaned forward and said, "We will *always* make sure you have everything you need, kitten. But how about this compromise—we'll send Libby and Charlie to your place to pack you a bag. They can get her things as well and then meet us out at the estate. We'll make sure everyone is careful around Libby, sweetness. Remember, we have as much or more to lose as you do. Now, why don't you let Trev help you find something in that wardrobe to wear while I make a couple of calls to get things set into motion? I'll be ready to go in five minutes." Trevlon watched as Jameson leaned forward and kissed her with the passion and hunger he knew wasn't going to be easily sated before he slowly turned her so Trev could pull her into his arms.

"God, baby, you feel so good snuggled in my arms—absolutely perfect. Let's get you a shirt to wear for the trip home. I promise you the car will be warm and you won't need anything more." The truth was, neither he nor Jameson would want her covered any more than necessary. It would take them at least an hour to make the trip and the time in the back of a nice warm limo would be used wisely.

Wrapping Kit in one of his own shirts had brought him a very strange sense of satisfaction. God she was so tiny the damned hem of the shirt fell well below her knees. He'd put her boots and clothes—well, what Jameson hadn't shredded—into a bag and sent them down to the car before they escorted her to their private elevator. As Trev had watched her walk down the hall in her bare feet and well-fucked hair, he'd had to fight the urge to howl like the wolf that he was. Jameson had smirked when he'd seen her. "Damn, kitten, we'll have to use the back stairs. Every man in the club would come in their pants if we walked you through looking like that." Shaking his head he made a quick call and then pulled her close once the elevators doors had closed. "The car will be waiting, it's only a few steps, but the concrete is too cold for those sweet feet so I'll carry you. We will always take care of you, kitten."

Trev could see the last hour and half was quickly catching up with Kit and she was fading fast. As soon as Jameson had settled her on his lap in the back of the limo, Trev pulled out a blanket and tucked it around her. They had barely gotten out of the parking garage when he'd looked over and watched her eyes flutter closed. Seeing her eyelashes brushing her cheeks and watching as her breathing even out when she fell deeper into sleep, Trev looked up and saw Jameson was watching her also.

Jameson's words described his own feelings perfectly. "She is amazing. I was beginning to think she was just a figment of our imaginations. I'm afraid to go to sleep for fear I'll wake up and find out it was all a dream. I've bought us a week. We have to convince her to stay because I know I'll never be able to let her go."

CHAPTER SIX

JAMESON COULDN'T REMEMBER a time when he had enjoyed the long drive to the estate as much as he had tonight. Holding his petite mate in his lap as she'd slept cuddled against his chest had been one of the most satisfying experiences of his life. He'd loved kissing her and fucking her had been a glimpse of heaven, but holding her like this—knowing she trusted him enough to sleep in his arms trumped all of the other great feelings, and wasn't that a kick in the pants. He smiled at Trev and then used their mind link to speak so they wouldn't disturb her. *'It humbles me that she is able to allow herself to be vulnerable in sleep while resting in my arms. I've set up everything at the estate. Many of the pack members wanted to meet her tonight but I've stalled them because I don't want her to feel overwhelmed. And I asked Charlie to take care of Libby and it sounded like he was more than happy to have an excuse to spend more time with her.'* He smiled when Kit's pink toenail polish reflected in the lights as they pulled up under the front awning near their home's front entrance.

Trev leaned over and pulled her small foot into his hand. "I hadn't even realized she'd gotten her feet out from under the blanket. God, her feet are so small and delicate. And that pink polish is going to be the end of me. Christ, her feet are so cold. We'll have to watch her, because I don't think she takes particularly good care of herself." Just then the limo door opened and the head of the estate staff and their right hand man, Tristan Michaels, was standing to the side waiting for them to exit the vehicle. Tristan wasn't as tall as Jameson and Trev but his weightlifters physique gave him an undeniable look of authority. They'd heard their friend described as intimidating more than once and had always laughed because that description was woefully inadequate.

Jameson carried their sleeping beauty straight into the house leaving Trev to give Tristan the instructions for the background check they wanted done on Kit. They had discussed the plan via their mind link earlier during the trip home. Jameson knew he and Trev were on the same page. They had agreed the information they got from the report wouldn't change the fact she was their mate, but it might help them know what was making her so reluctant to be mated. While he was fairly certain her reluctance wasn't about them specifically, he considered himself enough of a realist to recognize that knowledge was always power. And in the end, it was his responsibility to guard the safety of all the members of their pack. And even though the pack would always have to be their number one priority, he and Jameson would also move heaven and earth to protect their mate.

Jameson quickly made his way up the wide staircase and was grateful that Kit had stayed sleeping peacefully in his arms. He was all too aware of how intimidating their home would appear. For one thing the damned thing was fucking enormous, but hell, it needed to be when you took stock of how many members of their pack lived under one roof. For the most part, neither Jameson nor Trev ventured into the wings of the other family members unless they were specifically invited because they had always tried to view those areas with the same respect they would separate homes. Their own living quarters were actually made up of two floors and had always seemed like way too much space in his opinion. But right now he was thankful for the space because they'd have a nice spacious guest suite for Libby on the floor below their own bedroom suite. She'd be close—but not too close.

By the time he'd reached the door of the master suite, Trev had caught up and opened the door for them. Jameson smiled as he looked around the suite. "Remind me to thank whoever did this, bro." And then he leaned down and kissed Kit on the forehead, "Wake up, Sleeping Beauty. You've had a nice nap, but it's time to wake up and play." As she started to open her eyes, he nuzzled her neck, "Such a good girl. Open those beautiful eyes and look around. I'd say a couple of our pack members wanted to make sure you felt properly welcomed."

Watching as she blinked trying to bring the large room into focus, he set her gently on her feet but continued to hold on to her until she seemed stable. It was pure joy to watch as she took in her surroundings with child-like wonder. There were probably a hundred lit candles in the room and the smell of sage and citrus waltzed over his senses. But the thing that caught his eye was the large vases of fresh flowers sitting on several tables. The arrangements were beautiful but the defining feature of each was the prominent use of feathers. It struck him as an interesting choice until he watched Kit reach out and touch one of the feathers with a reverence that made him zero in on her every move. When she looked up at him with tears in her eyes, he stepped forward and pulled her into his arms. "Kitten, explain the tears, please."

"How did you know? I mean about the feathers? How

could you have possibly known?" her voice was almost child-like as she seemed completely stunned by the enormity of the gesture.

Trev had stepped up behind her and was running his fingers through her hair. "Tell us about the feathers, baby. We asked that our pack make you feel welcome and this is their gift to you. I'm glad it's meaningful, and I know my brother is as curious as I am about the significance of the feathers."

"As a child I was always searching for feathers. It made my father crazy and my mother swore it was a phase but my interest in them never seemed to fade. Finally my grandmother told them to back away from the subject because the feathers were my link to the Universe. She has told me thousands of times that when I found my mates they would be surrounded by feathers. She assured me several times that it was a clear signal that I was on the right path." Jameson watched as the tears she'd been trying to hold back slowly breached her lower lids and rolled leisurely down her flushed cheeks. When he leaned down and kissed them away, he savored the taste of them and wondered how they could be sweet and salty at the same time.

"Your grandmother sounds like a wonderful woman and we're anxious to meet her. But for this moment, I want to concentrate on getting you comfortable. Are you hungry, kitten?" He and Trev usually ate before they returned from the club, but he'd asked that their cook put a small tray of sandwiches in their suite's small kitchen so they wouldn't have to go to the main kitchen if Kit was hungry.

Jameson almost laughed out loud when she looked down and seemed to suddenly become aware of how little she was wearing. The sudden rush of pink flooding her cheeks was the most adorable thing he'd ever seen. "Well, yes, as a matter of fact I am a bit hungry, but I don't really want to go wandering about dressed like this. I don't want to embarrass you in front of your pack."

Jameson was thinking the same thing he heard echo from Trev via their mind link. *'Is she fucking serious? Embarrass us? Jesus, every unmated member of the pack will be walking around with a hard-on for her until we are mated.'* Trevlon was right, until they actually bit her and mixed their saliva with her blood to make her theirs she would attract a lot of attention, but it sure as hell wouldn't be the way she was thinking.

Trev turned her so she was facing him, "Baby, there is a tray of sandwiches in the small kitchen here in our suite. Come on. Let's get you fed before our shower. We'll all sleep better if we get the smell of the club off us before we climb into bed." Jameson watched as Trev led her from the room. She looked so tiny alongside his brother and for some odd reason that made him smile. Seeing her in one of their shirts and knowing she wasn't wearing a single thing under it was making him ache to slide his cock deep into her pussy again. Turning toward the bathroom he decided to make sure everything was set up because he knew Trev wouldn't be able to wait long either.

It was only a few short minutes before Trev led their sweet mate into the large spa bath. Jameson had turned on the heating coils they had embedded in the floor and since he'd already stripped down to just his leather pants he could feel the floor warming quickly beneath his bare feet. He smiled when he saw Kit flex her toes on the warm ceramic tile floor. "The floor is so warm, I love it. My feet get so cold and *oh my heavenly God.* This bathroom is unbelievable. And I thought my parents went over the top with theirs." She stopped and then grinned at them. "My mom's taste is garish. But this is perfect, it's a tropical paradise."

Jameson loved the master suite's bath, even though neither he nor Trev used it often. They had remodeled the entire suite almost a year ago in hopes their mate would enter their lives soon. Their housekeeper kept the plants looking perfect and everything fresh so their preparations this evening hadn't been too difficult. But whoever added the feathers to the floral arrangements was due a huge bonus. That was a given.

"I love the flora. You have captured the spirit of the rain forests of the Caribbean. The rock on the walls is perfectly asymmetrical and the texture shows a respect for Mother Nature's appreciation of randomness. The deep colors in the rock contrast with the earth tones used in the flooring." He and Trev were both barefoot and leaning against the vanity with their ankles crossed. He had his arms crossed over his chest watching Kit look around the room. When he glanced to his left, he realized Trev's pose mirrored his own. Jameson was enjoying her assessment of the room and it made each of the agonizing decisions the decorator had wrung out of them worth the time they'd taken. And when Kit seemed to realize they weren't answering, she suddenly turned and looked at them both. Her eyes went wide and he smiled when he saw her pupils dilate and her nostrils flare. *That's right, kitten. We want you again.*

"Come here, kitten." Jameson knew the steel in his tone would be unmistakable. He watched as she made her way toward him. When she was standing in front of him, he smiled down at her. "Such a good girl. Now, as much as

I enjoy seeing you in that shirt, I enjoy seeing you naked even more." When she didn't move he merely cocked his brow and looked at her expectantly.

"Baby, you do realize we are both Dominants, don't you?" Trev's question surprised him. It hadn't even occurred to him that she might have missed that point. But when she merely blinked and slowly nodded her head, Jameson was quite sure she didn't really understand what was implicit in the term. He smiled at Trev because he was sure his twin had the exact same thought. "Kit, tell me what you think that means."

The gorgeous sprite in front of them took a deep breath and sighed before squaring her shoulders. The first thing Jameson noted was that her voice had suddenly lost the airy quality it had when she was aroused. Hell, it was actually almost completely devoid of any affect whatsoever. "It means you want to be in charge. That you think you can boss me around and make me like it. Note that I didn't say it would work, I just said that is what you probably want to believe. I'm not a submissive. And if you want a weak-willed woman, I should probably just leave now and save us all the effort." Jameson saw a sadness flit through her expression that surprised him. Evidently she'd been hoping things would work out between them a bit more than she'd been willing to admit. Or perhaps she hadn't even been aware of how much she had been craving the feeling of connection that he knew she'd felt earlier when she'd been moving her tiny fingers over the feathers.

"Look at me, baby," Trev's voice was soft, but the command was still there. When she finally raised her eyes back up to meet his brother's, Jameson saw the raw desolation and loneliness she'd tried so hard to mask earlier.

"While it's true we will always be in charge in the bedroom, it is not true that we want a weak-willed woman. Where would the fun in that be?" Trev grinned at her and paused for a few seconds, giving her time to consider his words before continuing, "What we want is a woman who is strong enough to let us lead her to levels of pleasure she hasn't even begun to imagine exist. We want a woman who is brave enough to take a leap of faith and know we'll always be there to catch her if she falls. We want a woman who is fearless enough to tell us what she needs, whether it's advice, our help, a paddling, a cuddle, or to be fucked into next week." This time Trev's bad-boy grin cut through some of the tension that had been building and Jameson watched as Kit's shoulders seemed to relax a bit.

Jameson decided he'd been quiet long enough. He pushed off the vanity so he was now standing directly in front of her and he knew his height alone was intimidating. "The question is, kitten, are you brave enough to try? Or are you too afraid to go after what you want? Take off that shirt if you think you can handle this. Otherwise, we'll call it a night and discuss our options in the morning." He could hear his twin banging at the door of their mind link, no doubt pissed as hell that he'd shut it down for a few minutes.

He knew his words were a huge gamble, but he also knew Kit wasn't a coward and he'd seen the disappointment in her eyes a few minutes earlier when she'd thought it wasn't going to work. "Kitten, you don't really understand anything about our lifestyle. We know that and we're more than willing to show you. We'll also introduce you to some of the other women in the pack and I'm sure they'll be happy to tell you how much it adds to their lives rather than how much it takes away. We have several women who hold down very high ranking professional positions in the city, but they are also very contented, satisfied subs when they are here at home." He waited for several seconds and had to fight letting out a big sigh when her fingers slowly started opening the buttons on the front of the shirt she was wearing.

The minute he opened the mind-link, Trev was there. *'What the fuck was that about? I wanted to kick your ass, hell I still might just because I'm about to fucking drown in adrenaline. How did you know that would work? No, don't even tell me—you had no idea. Christ, I'm never playing poker with you again—Ever.'*

CHAPTER SEVEN

K IT WASN'T SURE what had possessed her to think she might be able to deal with these two. It had obviously been a moment of pure insanity. When she started opening the buttons on the shirt, she'd seen fire race through Jameson's eyes. Looking at Trev, she saw the same hunger, but his gaze was softer, more inviting even though she was sure he was every bit as commanding as his brother. But as her grandfather had always teased her *in for a penny, in for a pound,* so she took a deep breath and waited for their next instruction.

As it was, she didn't have to wait long. No sooner had the shirt hit the floor than Jameson's lips were crashing down on hers. The need she felt coming off him was chasing her own as the taste of him coursed through her. There was an edge of carnality underlying the urgency and she didn't fully understand why she'd recognized it or why it was appealing. When he let her up for air she felt herself being turned and then Trev's lips burned a similar hot seal of need into her. It was much like the brandings she'd heard her mother and grandmother discuss. And suddenly she understood their words had been only partially metaphorical because the heat rushing through Kit felt all too real to have been created in her mind.

When he finally pulled his lips from hers, she wondered, "I don't understand...how is it possible?" She hadn't meant to speak the words out loud, but she knew from the look on Trev's face she had done just that.

"What don't you understand, baby?" His voice was tender and the feel of his fingers moving along the sides of her face was drawing her deeper into a deep canyon of lust she feared she wasn't going to ever escape. When she just looked at him, trying to figure out how to answer without saying too much she felt his muscles go stiff against her. "Stop thinking of a way to answer without answering, Kit. Lying by omission is still lying and will not be allowed. The secret to successful matings is open and honest communication." He leaned down, kissed her forehead, and then continued, "Now, tell us."

Taking a deep breath, she laid her forehead against his bare chest and sighed. "My mother and grandmother are shifters, but they are also witches. They are a part of an extremely powerful coven that has been charged with protecting the world from the dark side. I've heard them talk about *brandings* and how witches are branded by their mates. I always thought they were either exaggerating or speaking figuratively. But, well…those last kisses with you both sent a heat through me that felt as if you were branding your names on my heart, and I was just trying to figure it out." She was actually really embarrassed at all she'd revealed in those few words and she was sure if they had really been listening, they would know exactly what she'd just told them.

Standing stock still, she was relieved when neither man moved for a few moments. They were obviously letting her get her feet back under her. When Jameson finally stepped up and pressed himself against her back, she felt him leaning down, the soft hair on his chest sliding over her back until his lips were against her ear. "Kitten, we intend to brand ourselves so deeply in you that you'll know until the end of time you belong to us. We have more questions about your mother and grandmother, but they aren't what you think. We're actually quite interested and looking forward to that conversation so don't let your concerns about that hold you back from us."

Kit didn't understand what he might want to ask her, but at this moment all she could think about was the fact that her senses were being nuked to oblivion by the men surrounding her. Their scents were almost more than she could deal with individually, but combined they were positively lethal to her self-control. She understood on an intellectual level the animalistic attraction was exactly that...animalistic. But that didn't explain the effect they seemed to be having on her heart. Nor did it shed any light on why she seemed to respond to them as Dominants. *Damn it, I'm not a submissive and I am too old for this shit. Why did I do this? Why am I here?*

JAMESON HAD BEEN patient long enough. There wasn't any doubt that his and Trev's connection to Kit was strengthening, because he knew she had only spoken some of her words aloud, but he'd heard them all, along with the underlying insecurities that had fueled them. But he wasn't going to let her sink into the hole of self-doubt he knew she was digging. He was anxious for her to spend some time with Julie and Angie. He knew his cousins would help Kit navigate the politics of pack-life as well as be great examples of how independent, professional women could find great satisfaction in their submission.

But until his fiery cousins could help, he and his brother were going to have to keep their hesitant kitten too busy and sated to let her mind wander into dangerous territory. Apparently there were a lot more layers to Ms. Kathleen Harris than most women, and he and Trev were going to have fun peeling back each and every one until they knew their mate even better than she knew herself.

"Kitten, your mind tends to block your pleasure and we'd like to teach you how to get past that, but you are going to have to help. Do you think you can do that?" He hadn't turned her to face him, choosing instead to lean down over her shoulder to whisper his words intimately against the soft hair covering her small ear. Gathering her curls in his hands, he wrapped it like a rope around his fist and tugged back gently. He wanted her to start recognizing her own physical and emotional reaction to their small moves of dominance and he was rewarded with her sharp intake of breath and the quaking shudder he saw move through her.

Moving Kit into the shower quickly, he smiled as she leaned her head back and let the rain shower overhead nozzles sluice warm water gently over her. Her every move was poetry in motion and Jameson found himself lost in a blissful haze of lust just from watching her. The water raced over her tight body—some of it washing down the curve of her breasts before launching itself off her peaked nipples, reminding him of the ski jumpers he'd watched last year in the Swiss Alps. But the more sensual water that was heavy with soap bubbles detoured and outlined the graceful curves of each breast before rejoining and going into a free-fall down her flat stomach and disappearing into the inviting folds of her sex.

Jameson could hardly wait to see her run through the hills on their estate in her wolf form. Since they had yet to claim her, he knew she hadn't ever shifted and she probably wasn't looking forward to it. He didn't know what her parents might have told her, but he and Trev would make sure she understood everything that was going to happen so her first shift wouldn't be as frightening as she expected. When he finally realized he'd been lost in thought as he watched bubbles teasing her bare pussy, he felt another wave of lust crash over him.

By the time Jameson brought his eyes back up, Trev was almost finished washing her hair and judging by her soft moans, Jameson guessed she was enjoying it a lot. Trev didn't try to hide the desire in his voice. "You like that, baby? I hear your heart beating faster and faster. Your breathing is becoming shallower and you arch into my touch. Let your sweet body lead your mind for a bit. You'll always be safe with us." Jameson smiled at Trev when Kit finally appeared to be letting her body push her mind aside. He couldn't wait to show her this was the very heart of submission. Letting her Masters control her pleasure, knowing they would protect and cherish her with everything in them. Yes, those were the gifts submission brought to the sub who was brave enough to let go and take that leap of faith.

Jameson stepped up in front of her and rolled her nipples between his fingers. His cock was already threatening to burst and they'd only just started. When she arched toward him, he took it as an invitation and leaned down, drawing first one and then the other pink bud into his mouth and lashing it with his tongue until he could smell her arousal. "I love the smell of your sweet cream, kitten. And I am thrilled to know your body is preparing itself to welcome us. Knowing your pussy is slick with liquid need is a very real turn on." Moving his fingers down to slide through her folds, he pulled her nipple between his teeth and pressed down just enough that she would get just a small bite of pain that would quickly be masked and then linked in her mind to the pleasure his fingers were building in her pussy.

Jameson knew when Trev moved her foot to the small stone bench along the shower wall what he had planned. When he heard his brother's words to her, he had to smile at her reaction. "Spread those beautiful legs, baby. I want to play a bit." When she gasped, Trev added, "Oh and Kit, don't come until one of us gives you permission." Jameson had pulled back and watched as her eyebrows rose in disbelief and then her eyes glazed over just before her knees folded.

Jameson had anticipated her drop just in time to pull her against his chest. "Easy, kitten, Trev just wants to play with your beautiful ass a bit. We'll need to stretch those tight muscles so you can take us both at the same time without it being too painful. We don't want to tear any of those delicate tissues." When he felt her stiffen in his hold, he added, "We won't be taking you together tonight, but we will soon. And I promise you, you are going to love it, we'll make sure you do."

She leaned back so she could look at him, her expression somewhere between anticipation and fear. Jameson just smiled at her and then asked, "Do you trust us, kitten? Does your heart know that we'd never hurt you?" He was relieved to see her nod her head and he felt more than saw her relax into his embrace. "Good girl, now lean on me and relax. Let Trev make you feel good, love."

When Jameson looked up at Trev, he saw the same love in his brother's eyes that he knew was shining in his own. Finding her had only been the tip of the iceberg.

Seeing the trust in her eyes as she gave over her body to them was filling places in his heart and soul he hadn't even known were empty. Sure, he and Trev had been looking for their mate, but only because they'd felt pressure to mate for the sake of the pack. And the spectacular woman in his arms was more than he could ever have hoped to find. This was bigger than just finding a mate to complete the family and carry their children—this was a connection that transcended simple love. There was something about this woman that held the answer to every dream he'd ever had, every fantasy he'd ever dared to allow to play out in his mind, and every wish he'd made late at night as he'd lain awake and alone.

CHAPTER EIGHT

TREVLON WOLF HAD never had to work very hard to get a woman into his bed and heaven knew he and Jameson had shared more than their fair share of willing subs over the years. But Kit was their mate so everything about this experience was amplified in significance and importance. When he'd moved her foot to the bench and then ran his fingers around the tight ring of muscles surrounding her anus to let her know he wanted to play, she had collapsed into Jameson's waiting arms. And for a heartbeat or two Trev had worried she was going to back out. But the warm wash of her arousal over his fingers let him know exactly how their words had affected her.

As Jameson had soothed her anxious reaction, he'd taken advantage of her distraction and begun pressing his finger gently into her rear hole. Part of their mating would involve them both claiming her in front of anyone in their pack who wanted to watch so it was important she understood exactly what pleasure awaited her on the other side of that first bit of pain. He didn't know how she would react when she discovered exactly how the ancient ceremony unfolded, but he knew they could make it so pleasurable she'd have long forgotten about their audience by the time they actually sunk their cocks into her.

"Push back against my finger, baby—just as you would if you were trying to push me out." He'd been using her thick cream as lubrication and his finger was slowly pressing again the ring of muscles that were tightly guarding her tight little ass. "Oh, sweet baby Jesus, she is so tight. That's it, baby, relax into it. I'm not going to hurt you and I promise this is going to launch you right over the moon."

Trev heard her panting breaths and knew she was getting close to her release so he leaned forward and gave her a small bite right on the plumpest part of her ass cheek. When he heard her moan against Jameson's chest, he knew she had been pulled back from the edge—even if it had been unwillingly. "Give yourself to me, Kit. Trust me to lead you and you won't be disappointed, I promise. Such a good girl, let Jameson hold you. Neither he nor I will ever let you fall. And right now, the only thing that you need to do is *feel*."

All the time he'd been speaking to her, Trev had been pushing his finger deeper and deeper into her anus and each bit of progress he was rewarded with sinfully sweet sounds of their mate closing in on a release he knew was going to rock all of them. Using his other hand, Trev moved his fingers through the slick folds of her pussy and started drawing circles around her clit. "Oh, please. I can't hold it, I swear I can't. It's too much…the wave is too big to hold back." Kit's voice was ragged with need and as a wolf, he could hear the vibrato of lust that normal human hearing would have missed.

Trev rotated the finger he had deep in her ass at the same time he pinched her pulsing clit and said, "Come for us, baby girl. Let it take you." Kit's body had reacted before his words could have possibly registered in her mind and the deep sense of satisfaction he felt in that knowledge surprised him. Her scream echoed off the shower walls and nearly made him come. From what he could see, his brother wasn't in much better shape.

Jameson held her through the aftershocks and Trev smiled as his brother whispered words of praise in her ear. They quickly finished their showers and worked together to dry Kit. Trev loved the fact her skin was still flushed from her release and he'd noticed the sparkles that they'd seen when they had fucked her at the club had been even brighter this time. He'd asked Tristan to do some research to see if he could find out more about the magical connection. Plus what the side effects of it might be.

Taking a wide-tooth comb with him into the bedroom, he sat on the small sofa in front of the stone fireplace at one end of the bedroom and opened his legs so Jameson could settle their petite princess in front of him. As Trev combed through her beautiful hair, he made sure he spoke in low tones so she was able to stay in the relaxed state as long as possible. As Doms, they both understood the importance of aftercare for subs and he seemed to instinctively know this was what Kit needed. Trev also knew it would be only a few minutes until they were all drowning in need and that despite the fact that she'd just come a few short minutes ago, there wasn't any doubt her delectable body was soon going to be on board for another round as well.

"Baby, your hair is the most amazing color I have ever seen. The reds are so varied and it looks like the Gods have woven in gold highlights that reflect each and every one of those shades." Trev was almost transfixed as he watched the colors lighten as her hair dried. The silken strands seem to almost transform right in his hands. As the waves became deeper, he couldn't seem to keep his hands from pulling the silken tresses through his fingers. "I can hardly wait to see these beautiful waves spread across my thighs as your lips wrap around my cock. And I'm going to relish the chance to wrap my fist in it and pull your sweet lips back to meet mine as I fuck you from behind." He emphasized his words by wrapping his hand in her still damp hair and pulling her back until he could run his tongue around the shell of her dainty ear.

By this time, Jameson was kneeling in front of her brushing his knuckles down the slope of her breast and just skimming her nipples. Trev watched as the fire of passion passed through Jameson's dark eyes. "I'm going to love walking you into the club with my hand just above your ass and feeling the soft tickle of these waves over my hand. I'll be able to run my fingers up your spine and when your whole body shivers at my touch, I'll brush your curls aside and nip at the tender spot where your neck joins your shoulder. Because, kitten, I already know that is a hot-spot for you—when you feel our touch there your whole body lights up with need."

Trev caught Jameson's quick nod to the bed just before he pulled Kit to her feet and led her to the enormous bed they had specially made for this room. Due to their height, their intent to share a mate, and their love of all things *kink*, they had ordered the bed and given the cousins who had created it some very detailed instructions. The end result was spectacular and everyone who had seen it had agreed it was truly a work of art. Bent metal scrollwork showing a forest scene with hidden wolves also concealed at least a hundred places to secure straps, cuffs, ropes, or chains. The head and footboards were joined overhead by framework, which concealed rolling beams that were remote controlled and had been designed for suspension play. And even though they had allowed the builders to show it to others as an example of their work, they had never had a woman in this bed because it had always been reserved exclusively for their mate. And their cousins had understood that once it had been used with their mate, it would no longer be shown to anyone for advertising.

Jameson had insisted their "mating bed" be held as a place of honor. Trev had thought his brother was being a bit of a drama-queen at the time—but he certainly did appreciate Jameson's foresight now. Hell, the idea of any other man seeing the bed where they fucked Kit almost made Trev insane with jealousy. Even their housekeeping staff was only going to be given limited access to the master suite for several days. As the Alphas of their pack, they were the equivalent of the President and Vice-President of a small nation, and the desire for gossip was always a problem for men in powerful positions, no matter the circumstances. The thought of having Kit hurt by pack gossip was almost enough to make him physically ill.

Once they'd settled Kit on the bed, Trev smiled as her eyes seemed to be focusing enough to realize at least some of the special features of the bed. He leaned over and spoke against soft lips swollen from their kisses. "Baby, we're going to show you every single *extra* we had added to the bed that has been waiting unused until we found our mate—but that little *tour de bed* needs to wait until later, because right now Jameson and I need to fuck you, sweetness."

Jameson had knelt next to her head and was slowly stroking his cock from root to tip and Trev watched as she turned her attention to him. When her pink tongue licked her lower lip, Trev heard Jameson's groaned, "Fuck." And when she used the tip of her tongue like a tiny scoop to retrieve the pre-cum that was filling the slit at the end, Jameson growled "God, woman, you're going to be the death of me. Open and take me in. That's it—use your tongue to feel how hard you make me. I want you to take me as deep as you can. Good girl, breathe through your nose." Jameson's words were sounding awfully strained and Trev couldn't help but smile about that fact. His brother was known among subs as being able to hold off his own release for hours while playing with them. And now the Dom known for his mastery of his own body was being tossed over in minutes by a tiny little redhead who up until a couple of hours ago had been a virgin.

Trev had watched as long as he could but as hot as it was to see Kit learning how to bring one of her mates to the edge of his control, it was time to join in the fun. Jameson's growled words through their mind link letting Trev know that if he wanted to join the party, he needed to get with it. He rolled over her in one smooth move and used his knees to spread her legs as far apart as they would go without being secured. He leaned down so his lips were pushing against her ear and whispered, "Are you wet for me, baby? Let's see, shall we?" Before she could react to his question, he thrust deep into her hot channel and froze when he felt the walls of her vagina start rippling around him. "Oh no you don't, baby—you don't get to come again just yet. I want to slide in and out, and feel your hungry pussy gripping me as you try to keep me inside of you." In truth he wasn't sure how long he was going to last and from the sounds he heard coming from deep in Jameson's chest, he was skating on the edge as well.

Kit was groaning around Jameson's cock and Trev could see beads of sweat trickling down the sides of his brother's face. "Oh, sweetness, you certainly are testing our ability to maintain our control." Then looking up at his brother, he added, "And brother, I do believe she is doing it on purpose. What should we do about this? Seems like she is trying to top from the bottom if you ask me." Trev opened the mind link, *'I think we need to flip her over and let her continue to suck you and I'll give her a couple of swats and see how she reacts.'* Jameson's nod was immediate and affirmative.

KIT DIDN'T HAVE any idea what was going on. *What the hell did they mean topping from the bottom?* But she was a whole lot less than thrilled when Jameson pulled his cock past her lips and Trev withdrew from her pussy. She was suddenly feeling very empty and very pissy about it. "What the hell? Did I do something wrong? If I'm not playing this sucky-fucky game to suit you, perhaps you could cut me a bit of slack here. I mean after all I'm pretty new to this and even though I'm older than most women you know…hell, I'll bet I'm older than *anybody* you know…that doesn't mean I have played these games before."

Oh boy, she was on a roll now. She was amazed at how frustrated she felt about being denied another orgasm. It seemed like tormenting a child by taking away a toy she'd just been given if you asked Kit. And the more she talked the more frustrated she became and the more she spoke her mind. "Well fairies and lightning bugs, this sucks I tell ya. Give me a new toy and then take it back. Fuck a duck that is just plain mean."

She was all too aware that both Jameson and Trev dwarfed her. However, she hadn't really felt tiny or over-powered until Trev wrapped his hands around her waist, completely encircling it before lifting her off the bed and flipping her over onto the pillows Jameson had quickly positioned under her lower abdomen, which left her bare ass pointing to the ceiling. When she started scrambling to get back up, she felt Jameson's hands pull her arms out in front of her. His enormous bear paw hands easily wrapped around both of her wrists and held her pinned to the bed. But it was his snarled, "Stop" that had her freezing in place.

She felt her pussy flood with cream and the fact she had responded to Sir Bossiness just served to piss her off even more. Just as she was working to figure out what they were up to, she felt a sharp slap on her ass. "Hey! What the hell was that for? I'm not the one who is being a jerk here. You need to put your hands on somebody else's ass, and find some woman who likes to play your little slap and tickle games, because I am outta here." She once again tried to pull her hands free from Jameson's manacle grip.

Jameson leaned down close to her ear and growled at her. "Stop fighting *and talking* before you dig yourself any deeper, kitten. We were just going to play with you a bit to see how you react to an erotic spanking, but now you've earned yourself some punishment swats with that little tirade you just let fly. We'll discuss what that was about later, but right now Trev is going to paddle your ass until it's a nice bright shade of crimson. You'll learn to watch your tone and keep your words sweet or you'll figure out how to function without sitting down comfortably until you master the skill. And believe me when I tell you, every single pack member you meet tomorrow is going to know exactly why you are squirming in your seat at dinner."

Just as Jameson stopped talking, Trev rained swats over every square inch of her ass. He never struck the same place twice in a row and he varied the intensity enough that she couldn't anticipate or mentally prepare for the next stroke. And much to her mortification her pussy seemed to be more than a little enthused by the whole plan. When he finally stopped and slid his fingers through the pulsing lips of her pussy, she moaned and tried to press herself into his touch. She felt him rubbing his other hand lightly up and back down the length of her spine and his voice was raspy with need when he spoke to her. "Oh, sweetheart, I don't think you want to protest that paddling too much—not the way your pussy is soaking wet and you were lifting this beautifully paddled ass into my strokes."

She had become so lost in the strangeness of the entire thing, she had barely registered that he'd stopped spanking her until she felt his fingers push deep into her. "Oh, please. Please don't stop. It feels so good and I want you inside me so much...and I don't understand why, but having your body inside mine is the most amazing thing...and I'm so very close, please let me come." Kit knew her words were slightly slurred but she was having so much trouble focusing that it just didn't seem important enough to try to correct.

"Turn to me, kitten, and suck me down that tight little throat of yours. Fuck, I almost came watching you get your ass swatted. Seeing how your body responded to that bite of pain was the hottest thing I've ever seen in my entire life. That's it, keep your mouth open and let me fuck it. When I come I want you to swallow every drop, do you hear me? Every fucking drop, Kit."

Kit's mind was mush, she heard Jameson's words but her body was on autopilot. And just as he pushed deep into her mouth, Trev drove his rock hard length all the way into her sheath and she was sure she could feel the head pressing against the inside of her navel. Trev had folded himself over her, his lower abdomen was pressed against her heated ass and they both took full advantage of her started gasp.

"You best learn to keep that sharp tongue of yours in check, baby, or you'll get spankings until you do. As our mate, you will be expected to set an example." He was fucking her with long, slow, deep thrusts timed with his words and she was barely registering that he was even speaking let alone what the words meant. "Now, sweet mate, I want you to listen closely to my words. Are you listening, Kit?"

She wondered how she was supposed to listen when she was so close to losing herself in the torrent of sensations they were creating. She was overwhelmed by the feeling of Jameson's hard, veined cock sliding over her lips as they stretched to accommodate his girth and Trev's cock caressing a spot inside her that felt like someone had just turned on all the lights on the Rockefeller Center Christmas tree. She finally managed to nod her head and then tightened her lips around Jameson's cock and squeezed her vaginal muscles as tightly as she could as Trev pulled from her once again. She was pleased to hear Jameson and Trev both groan.

"Fuck, baby, that feels unbelievable. Jesus, Joseph, and Mary you are so tight. Listen to me, baby, when your Alpha shoots his seed into your sweet mouth you'll swallow it down—every drop. And then put your face back down on the mattress and open that pussy up to my possession."

She felt the rhythm of their cocks moving in and out of her body, but she also felt as if she was floating somewhere over the bed watching as the most erotic scene she'd ever imagined played out before her. Just as she started to worry she wasn't going to be able to hold off her release any longer, she heard Jameson's shout and immediately felt the warm pulses of his salty essence coating her tongue and throat. She'd never tasted a man's semen before and she knew she was going to become addicted to the taste of these two men, and that was comforting and terrifying at the same time.

When Jameson pulled from her mouth he leaned down and kissed her forehead, "That was amazing, kitten. Watching my cock slide into your sweet mouth and then knowing you were greedily swallowing my seed nearly turned my heart inside out. Now lay flat and let Trev take you on a magic carpet ride." Listening to Jameson's words of praise and direction turned out to be the last cognitive thought Kit was able to muster.

CHAPTER NINE

WATCHING KIT'S MOUTH open itself to Jameson's pleasure was almost enough to make Trev lose his own control. And seeing her push forward so he knew his brother's cock had to be pushing into her throat had him aching to take her sweet mouth as well. Resuming his strokes as soon as Jameson had her settled, Trev knew he was building her need to a frenzied level and that was exactly what he wanted to do. He knew by making sure the only thing predictable about his strokes was the fact he'd kept everything totally random was going to help him bring her to an electrifying peak.

"The feeling of your hot pussy creaming around me, trying to pull me back in each time I pull back, is the most exquisite torture I've ever known." It was taking every last ounce of his self-control to not lean down the length of her slender back and sink his teeth into the top of her shoulder—mixing their DNA into her blood and claiming her. But she hadn't agreed *yet* and he and Jameson had always planned on claiming their mate together. For now filling her with a pleasure so earthshattering it bound her heart to his would have to be enough, that and the satisfaction of knowing he was going to be shooting his seed as deep in her as it could possibly go.

Trev leaned over Kit and moved her hair aside so his tongue could lick the outer curve of her ear. Running his hand under her and down her flat stomach, he felt her muscles rippling in their desperate need to orgasm. Then his fingers trailed further down and found her clit standing out from its hood as if it had been awaiting his arrival. He circled the small bundle of nerves twice before pinching it as he commanded her, "Come for me, baby. Come *now!*"

He felt her entire body stiffen and then her pussy locked down on him like a living vice and he growled as she pulled him right over the edge with her. Trev would have sworn all the tales he'd heard about flashing lights and bursts of color his friends had described had been nothing but wishful, created memories, but *this*? This had made a believer out of him. When he'd felt his mate's channel flood with the cream of her release he'd lost his mind to the pleasure and come so hard he'd been worried he was going to lose all muscle control and collapse right on top of her dainty little frame. How he'd managed to keep from doing exactly that was nothing short of a miracle because she'd drained him of every rational thought and most of his energy as well.

As he lay propped over her, panting for breath and try-ing to clear the fog from his brain, he felt the bed shift and knew Jameson was going to the bathroom and would be starting the hot tub so they could take care of their mate. But it was going to be a few minutes before everything was ready and that bit of time would hopefully be enough to get his muscles and brain to begin working together again. He'd been with his share of women over the years, but none had decimated him like Kathleen Harris. Oh indeed, their mate was going to own every inch of their hearts and souls—probably before they even got to claim her.

When he'd finally regained his voice and could actually hear again once the blood stopped pounding in his ears, he leaned down and kissed her ear. "Baby, are you okay? I didn't hurt you did I?"

Hearing her sniffed, "No, I'm fine" almost stopped his heart. He quickly rolled her so he could see the tears rolling over her perfect cheekbones. He knew she would see the alarm in his eyes, but he didn't care. If he'd hurt her, he wasn't sure he'd ever be able to forgive himself. She must have sensed how frantic he was because she raised her delicate fingers and ran them gently down the side of his face. "I don't know why I'm crying, it was just so...intense that it touched a place so deep in my soul...a place I didn't even know existed. And...well, it was a bit overwhelming."

Trev pulled her into his arms and just held her against his chest, saying a silent prayer of thanks to the keeper of the stars for sending her into their path. He and Jameson had waited so long for her and now that he held her, he wasn't sure he'd ever sleep again unless she was nestled safely between him and his brother.

There was no doubt that Jameson had felt the pressure of finding their mate even more than Trevlon had. Mating was expected of every member of the pack, but the mating of the pack Alpha was always highly anticipated. Because of their longer than usual lifespans and the fact that matings were for life combined to mean that these events didn't happen that often, so theirs was sure to garner a lot of attention.

"Baby, emotion isn't something we ever want you to hide from us. And what we all just experienced was very powerful so we aren't surprised or alarmed by your tears. Please don't try to hold that back from us because holding back feelings of any type is a slippery slope that can only lead to feelings of disconnection." Looking deeply into her eyes, Trev watched as a spark of realization seemed to ignite. *That's right, sweetheart, you belong to us and that means we want each and every piece that makes you who you are. There can be no secrets.*

When she finally nodded in understanding, he stood, scooped her into his arms, and made his way into the bath. Jameson had already added bath salts that would hopefully soothe the muscles he was sure would be aching by morning without some tender aftercare on their part. Lifting her over the edge of the bubbling tub, Trev set her on Jameson's lap before climbing in himself. Trev leaned back and watched as Kit curled into his twin's chest just like the kitten Jameson called her.

'She is so beautiful and so deeply submissive, whether she admits it or not. Did you see the way she was arching into my hand?' Trev noticed their mind link was growing stronger each time they fucked Kit and wondered again at the deepening of the connection. He had been under the impression their link would strengthen after mating, so now he had to wonder just how much stronger it might get.

Jameson answered, but never took his eyes off the woman sated and now sleeping in his arms. *'I can't wait to show her everything—the strength of our bond surprises me since we have only had her in our lives a few hours. And my desire to fuck her again grows by the minute even though I can see she is utterly exhausted. I can hardly wait for her to meet the other women and to find out how strong matings are. I want her to fully understand the depth of the relationships between mates, and how honored and cherished she'll always be. We have to make this work, I won't ever be able to let her go.'*

The look in Jameson's eyes when he lifted his gaze to meet his own was something between fierce protector and lovesick romantic. And just for a heartbeat, Trev saw vulnerability in Jameson's eyes that he hadn't seen since the night their parents had died. Sighing to himself, Trev just moved his eyes back down in a soft caress over Kit. "Come on, let's get her dried and into bed. She is so tired and we need to have her sleeping between us if we're going to follow our own rules and begin as we intend to go."

After they'd dried their very sleepy mate and settled her between them, Trev pulled her close and kissed her forehead before settling her against his chest. When Jameson crawled in on her other side, he growled, "Keep her between us, brother. I am not sleeping up against your hairy ass. Fuck, I'll probably have nightmares just thinking about it. And you can hold her for a while, but then send her my way."

Trev tried to unsuccessfully to hold in his snort of laughter when their very sleepy bed partner spoke up, "I'm not a toy you boys can fight over, you know. But I will admit it feels mighty fine being held by you both. But don't start thinking I'm just going to roll over and spread my legs for you anytime you demand it...although the idea does hold more appeal than I thought it might. Boy oh boy, sure hope my parents don't get wind of this..."

Smiling over at Jameson, Trev watched as his brother leaned over and gently bit down on the top of Kit's shoulder. "Why is that, kitten?" They both knew she had been talking in her sleep and likely hadn't intended to give away quite so much information.

Kit's soft sigh against his chest went straight to his cock. Trying to hold his libido in check, Trev held perfectly still waiting for her to answer Jameson's question. "Oh, you know, they have been pushing for me to find my mates for so long. And Granny Good Witch will probably tell them, hell that crazy geriatric commando knows everything." She burrowed closer and then took a deep breath in through her nose, "Oh, Trev, you smell so good. I can tell you apart by smell alone. Jameson smells good too, but more like the woods after a spring rain. But you smell like a warm day at the beach. Remember, don't tell Richard or Carla. I'm so tired…going to sleep a bit now."

Trev was thrilled to have found out her parent's names, he smiled as Jameson slipped quietly out of the bed. Knowing her parents would be in favor of their mating would be to their advantage, because despite what the tiny beauty in his arms wanted them to think, it was obvious she valued her parents' opinion. *Rest, my sweet baby, you are safe in my arms forever.*

CHAPTER TEN

J AMESON WAS ALREADY dialing before he had even gotten the door of the bedroom closed. He knew Kit hadn't meant to disclose so much information, but keeping her was much more important at this point than playing fair. Letting her go was just not an option and if it took recruiting the help of her parents, then that was exactly what they'd do. Besides, he was more than a little anxious to speak with Carla Harris anyway. The thought that Kit's mother was the witch who had fought so bravely trying to defend his and Trev's parents just wouldn't leave the back of his mind.

Tristan answered on the first ring and Jameson could tell by the noises he heard in the background he'd caught their Chief of Staff before he'd left his office which meant Angie must be working late at the hospital. After he'd given Tristan all of the information, he asked, "Did Angie get called in?"

"Yes. Sounds like there was a big blow-up downtown—near the club actually—when they called her in they gave her the impression the circumstances of the explosion were suspicious. Hell if you ask me, if you have an explosion in downtown New York City it's a given that it's suspicious. Wait, hang on a minute. Let me cross-check something." Jameson waited several long minutes before hearing Tristan's soft curses. "Hey, man, we may have a big problem. Seems that explosion was in a rather spacious apartment rented by your woman. And yes I know her name isn't all that unusual so I ran it through and got everything—it's your girl alright. There isn't anything left by the way and the young boy that was injured lived across the hall and happened to be opening the door into the hall when her apartment went up like some kind of Fourth of July spectacular."

Jameson heard his friend shifting and then his whole demeanor seemed to have changed, "Hey, I'm sorry, that was really insensitive of me. And when you tell Kit, please tell her the boy is going to be okay according to Angie. I just sent her a message asking because I thought Kit might wonder about him. Ang says the parents have been worried about Kit. I hope you don't mind, but I asked Angie to discreetly tell them that she is safe. It doesn't sound like they need any additional worries."

"No, that's fine. Fuck, if they are worried about Kit that means she is going to know them and feel awful for the child. Any idea what happened in her apartment? Gas explosion?" The hair on the back of Jameson's neck was standing up and he was relieved that Libby and Charlie had arrived safely at the estate over an hour ago. He was hoping his sixth sense was off center this time, but somehow he didn't think that was the case.

"I can't get anything yet, but we've got people on the inside so I'll work on it. Get some rest, boss, and maybe you can hold off talking to Kit about this until tomorrow since I doubt you'll have the television on much up there." Jameson could hear the laughter in his friend's tone and knew he was trying to lighten his mood.

"I'll set my phone to silent, so text me if you get anything. And let's kick up the perimeter security until we get something that tells us this wasn't directed at Kit specifically. I have to tell you, I don't have a good feeling about this. If you need me quickly, send up someone discreetly." After saying their goodbyes, Jameson headed back upstairs. When he opened the bedroom door, he found the two most important people in the world sleeping peacefully wrapped in each other's arms. Standing alongside the bed he watched as their bodies seemed to have aligned themselves to the same heartbeat and Jameson felt a level of contentment he hadn't known since long before he'd lost his parents. Climbing in behind Kit, he was surprised when she turned toward him and opened her sleepy eyes. He could see she was having trouble focusing and he leaned forward and placed kisses on both of her eyelids, "Go back to sleep, kitten."

Her light, airy voice didn't sound anything like the woman who had, just a short time ago, been filled with frustration and fire. "I was starting to worry about you. Is everything alright?" Jameson tried to relax his body against hers, hoping she would let it go and fall back to sleep. Instead, she seemed to come more fully awake and pulled back until she was able to meet his gaze. "Jameson?"

That one word question let him know he only had two options. He could tell her what he knew she would much rather hear or he could tell her the truth. And as much as he knew he should tell her exactly what he'd learned, there was still a part of him that wanted to protect her from anything that would hurt her. He wasn't fool enough to fall for the hard-ass attitude she'd tried to pass off a couple of times since they'd met her. No, he knew there was a very fragile woman beneath the "bad-girl persona" and flip attitude. And he hated the fact he was going to send an arrow straight into her heart. *Fucking hell, not the way I wanted this night to end.*

Jameson sat on the bed and leaned his back against the headboard, "Come here." He was pleased when she immediately crawled into his lap and let him spend a few moments just finger combing her hair. The move was probably more about soothing his own soul than hers, but so be it. When he looked down he saw Trev's eyes were on him and his twin knew there was something wrong, but he was waiting patiently for the information.

"First of all, can you tell me what your relationship is with the family that lived across the hall from you?" The minute the words left his mouth, Jameson realized his mistake, but it was too late to correct the error.

"Lived? As in past tense? What does that mean?" And just as expected she hadn't missed his slip of the tongue and was now fully alert. Gone was the sexy sleepy goddess he'd come back into the room to find resting so beautifully in his brother's loving embrace. In her place was a wide-eyed, very worried woman who obviously had at least a passing friendship with a child who was lying in a hospital injured because he'd had the misfortune to open his front door at the wrong moment.

"There was an explosion in your building tonight, kitten. Well, more specifically, there was an explosion in your apartment. The young boy that lives across the hall from you was injured when he opened his front door just before the blast." He saw her eyes go wide in alarm a split second before they filled with heartbreak and tears. "Kitten, he is going to be okay. One of our pack members is a pediatric surgeon and she was called in tonight to treat him. And while I don't know the specifics of his injuries, I did speak with Tristan a few minutes ago and he had contacted Angie and she assured him that he is going to be fine." He could tell by her expression she was having trouble figuring out exactly who was who in the zoo and since they hadn't introduced her to Tristan on the way in, he wasn't even sure where to start.

"I'm so confused and but all I can think about is little Dusty. Are you sure he is going to be alright? I'm not usually a big hit with kids, but he has stolen my heart because for some reason he seems to really like me. Thinking he's been hurt because of a problem in my home is almost too much to take in." Christ, Jameson hadn't wanted to do this and the sad expression in her eyes was going to haunt him for years.

"The family was concerned about you and I gave Tristan permission to let the family know that you are safe here—none of us felt they needed anything else to worry about—I hope that is alright with you." He had been sure it would be fine and her quick nod was confirmation.

"Now that you know your pint-sized friend is going to be fine, I want to ask you, do you have any idea who might want to destroy your apartment or hurt you?" He saw the confusion in her expression and watched as it changed to a slow realization.

"Is there anything left in my apartment? Was that where the blast originated? Oh my God, no one thinks I did anything to cause that do they?" The panic in her voice was starting to concern him, but her hyperventilating needed to be addressed first.

Trev got up, sat next to him, and pulled Kit's legs over his lap. Leaning forward he pulled her chin up, capturing it between his fingers so she was looking into his eyes. "Breathe with me, baby. In nice and slow and out just as calmly. Good girl, again." Jameson watched as Trev worked to bring Kit's breathing under control. When she finally seemed to be back on an even keel, Trev leaned forward and kissed her on the end of her nose. "Such a good girl. Now, let's get the rest of this story, okay?"

She slowly nodded and brought her attention back to Jameson. "No, I really don't know why anyone would want to hurt me. It's not as if I'm anyone special or anything. I've lived there for quite a while and have never had any problems with anyone. As you can imagine, I try to fly under people's radar for the most part because I don't want to draw any unwanted attention. The family across the hall are the only people besides Libby...*Oh my God*...is Libby alright? Please tell me she and your friend, Charlie, weren't in my apartment when this happened."

"They are fine, kitten. They had already left when this happened. I'm sure if they had seen anything unusual, they would have alerted someone. We'll check with them in the morning. Please continue with what you were saying." Jameson hadn't been surprised when she finally remembered he'd sent someone to her apartment to get things she might need.

"Thank heaven. Okay, I just wanted to say the family across the hall and Libby are the only outside visitors I've ever had. My parents and grandmother have been there, but that is all. And while my mother and grandmother do leave 'trace magic' behind, someone would have to be magical themselves to pick it up or at least to identify it." Jameson was glad to see Kit seemed to have snapped back to herself and she was obviously giving his questions and concerns a lot of thoughtful consideration. "I don't re-member seeing anyone out of the ordinary around recently and my family hasn't been to visit in quite some time. I do know the building security finally did notice that each time my mom came around their electronics systems went on the fritz but most of that is her playing with them."

She must have noticed he and Trev's confused looks because she added, "My mom is a very…very beautiful woman, but she is also insanely *peculiar* about having her photograph taken, so…she tends to muck up surveillance equipment purposefully so there are no pictures of her floating about." Kit seemed to shrug it off, but Jameson went instantly on alert.

'I agree, brother, Kit's mom doesn't want her face out in cyber-space for reasons other than simple vanity.' Trev's voice had just spoken what Jameson had been thinking himself. But the real question was why. Unless she was a much more powerful force than they were being led to believe, because even though Kit had said her mother and grand-mother were a part of a powerful coven she hadn't referred to them specifically as powerful. And since Jameson hadn't detected any deception in Kit's voice when she'd spoken about the two of them, he was fairly certain Carla Harris's daughter probably didn't know all that much about her mother's or her grandmother's activities or their spheres of influence.

Hugging her tightly against him, he asked, "Do you think maybe you could manage to get a bit of sleep, sweetheart? We want to be able to introduce you to our friends tomorrow, they'll be dying to meet you and we know you've had a really big day."

At her slow nod, they slid down and positioned her between them. Jameson was surprised to see her eyes slide closed almost immediately and her breathing even out as she fell into a deep sleep. Trev's words echoed his own concern, "I'm worried about her safety. There is just this niggling feeling in the back of my mind that says she was the target tonight. What I can't figure out is why would anyone want to hurt her? And the significance of it occur-ring the first night we meet her has me wondering if someone isn't trying to keep us apart."

Jameson had just started considering the same possibil-ity and there wasn't any way to paint it that was good. "I've already asked that our perimeter patrols be stepped up and we'll need to review our electronics as well. I agree with you, someone knows a lot more about our mate than we know and that just plain pisses me off."

CHAPTER ELEVEN

K IT FELT LIKE she was slowly surfacing from hibernation. For a few seconds she just lay with her eyes closed and enjoyed the feeling of the sheets as they slid over her bare skin...*Bare?* Oh brother, she was wide awake now. She didn't ever sleep naked so something was seriously wrong with this picture. Jerking up in the bed she realized she was alone in the biggest bed she'd ever seen and just that fast, everything came rushing back to her conscious mind. And right on the tails of blushing at the memories of all the pleasure she'd been given was a crashing wave of sadness at the news little Dusty had been hurt and everything she owned blown to bits.

Turning her gaze to the large windows in the bedroom, she found her thoughts lost in the beauty of the gardens below. Looking around until she found one of the men's shirts discarded over the back of a chair, she quickly buttoned the middle two buttons and moved to stand before the windows and take in the winter wonderland outside. *Damn, told Libby it was going to snow, but did she listen to me? Oh hell no, and now here we are out here in the country without winter wear.* Sighing to herself, Kit couldn't help feeling a bit of loss at the things in her apartment she'd never see again. She didn't collect anything, but she had gotten a few nice pieces of jewelry from her grandfather before he'd passed away last year and thinking about those being gone brought tears to her eyes.

She shivered involuntarily just as she was wrapped in a warm embrace and pulled back against the solid wall of Trev's chest. "Tell me what's put the sad look in your beautiful eyes, baby. Seeing you hurting is painful for me as well." She didn't want to seem weak but in this moment, she just couldn't help but turn in his arms and rest in his care. Kit didn't cry often because, it had always seemed like a huge waste of energy if you asked her, but she just let the tears flow silently and hoped they would help purge the sadness that had snuck up on her. When Trev picked her up in his arms and made his way to the small sofa, she just curled into his lap and let his warmth surround her. She didn't really understand much about matings, but if this feeling of comfort was a part of the deal, she might have to reevaluate her objections.

Feeling Trev's hand tracing symbols on her back, she stilled for a moment and paid attention until she could identify them. "Those are rune symbols of protection aren't they?"

Kit wasn't sure Trev had heard her at first, but she felt him take a deep breath just as he'd finished the last of what she knew was a series. "Yes, baby, that is exactly what they are. Jameson and I learned them the night our parents all died. Our mom traced them into each of our hands and over our hearts before she and our dads locked us in a closet to keep us safe. She must have put a spell on the door as well, because by the time we could finally get the door open it was too late." When she looked up at him she knew he'd read the confusion in her eyes. "Keep in mind we were already young men and quite large for our age, so keeping us contained would have been impossible without magic. The symbols and magic were the final gestures of love we saw, but I'm sure our wonderful mother died, instead of letting us help our fathers protect her."

She just kept quiet because she could sense he wasn't finished with his story and she didn't want to interrupt.

When he finally seemed to come back into the moment, he looked at her and for a brief moment, she saw the young man he'd been when he'd lost his parents and she saw a flash of how hard he and Jameson had fought trying to get free so they could help. Trev leaned forward and kissed her so sweetly on the forehead, and said, "I hadn't used them again until last night with you."

"Why? I mean why last night?" She remembered him tracing on her skin, but she'd been so overwhelmed at the moment with lust, she hadn't taken time to identify what he'd done.

"I don't really know, it just came over me and from what we have learned this morning that was at almost the exact time your apartment was being wired to blow by two men who successfully conned your doorman into letting them in your apartment with some bogus story about delivering a computer. Our best guess is they used some sort of magic because when police interviewed the doorman last night he seemed completely baffled about why he'd fallen for something that was so obviously a lie."

Kit felt Trev shift just before he stood her on her feet. "Now, the reason I'm here is to make sure you are up and functional. We need to get you showered and dressed quickly so we can make the meeting in our office downstairs. So get a move on, baby. While you are in the shower, I'll bring in the bag Libby packed for you. And before you ask, Charlie and Libby have already left to go snowmobiling so you don't have to worry about answering any of her questions just yet."

Kit squeaked when he gave her still tender ass a sharp swat, which sent her scurrying into the bathroom. She quickly took care of all her morning routine and was back out in the bedroom searching for her clothing in short order. The towel she'd wrapped around her was huge so she hadn't thought anything about exiting the bath with nothing but it wrapped around her. She regretted the move as soon as she stepped in to the room and heard Jameson's growled, "Kit" just before he shoved her back into the bathroom. *What the hell?*

At her startled look he said, "Didn't you notice there were people in the room, mate?" *What crawled up his ass this morning? And hell no she hadn't noticed because the only thing she'd seen was his large self and his snarly, pissy expression.* "Pissy expression? Oh sweet kitten, I'll show you pissy. And yes, you did indeed speak those thoughts out loud. Now, we have security people out there installing some extra precautions and I'd prefer they didn't get to see our mate's glorious body wrapped in nothing but a towel." She saw Trev was standing just outside the door and knew there was something Jameson wasn't telling her, but she also knew better than to push either of them at this moment. Hell, she could barely sit now without wincing so adding any more fire to her ass didn't seem like a very wise choice.

KIT HAD GONE from relaxed and sated to flaming in the blink of an eye. "Well alrighty then. All you had to do was let me know and I'd have been thrilled to sit in here all day waiting for someone to bring me something to wear." Boy oh boy she was working on a good-mad now so she might as well go down fighting. "And furthermore, I'm not your mate. One night of sex...okay, it was really amazing sex...but still, one night of sex doesn't mean we're mates because I have to tell you, right now I'm kind of thinking you're an asshat." She was pretty sure she saw the corner of his mouth twitch just before they both heard a chuckle from the other side of the door.

When Trev opened the door and stepped in, he didn't do a thing to hide his amusement. "Well, brother, I see you are doing a great job of pissing off the most beautiful woman in the world. Christ, I leave you alone with her for two minutes and you have her spitting mad like the kitten you call her." He stepped up and handed Kit the clothes he'd brought for her. He must have seen her mentally inventorying what he'd handed her because when she looked up at him and opened her mouth to ask, he'd just smiled and placed his finger over her lips to keep her from speaking before chuckling, "No, baby, I didn't forget anything. That is exactly what we want you to wear and if you kick up a fuss, you'll be wearing a few hand prints and tender bare ass as well."

Kit wanted to snap back but figured this was one of those "choose your battles" moments she was always hearing her mom talk about. She took a deep breath and nodded at Trev before glaring at Jameson. When neither one seemed like they were planning to leave anytime soon she sighed and dropped the towel before sliding the dress over her head. The knit was clingy and did nothing to hide her tightly peaked nipples. And the feel of the silky fabric washing over her skin in soft waves felt so much more sensual without underwear. But crap if she had to be in a meeting without underwear that was going to be seriously distracting and getting wet and having a big wet spot on the back of her dress was really going to make a great impression on their pack members.

When she finally realized they were both grinning at her like loons she rolled her eyes and groaned, "Please tell me I didn't do it again. *Frack it.* I really have to stop speaking out loud. It's like giving looters the keys to the kingdom. Damn."

Jameson and Trev both laughed out loud and surrounded her. "Looters are we, kitten? Well then, I'll guess we'll have to see what treasures we've scored as soon as we get this meeting done. And I'm sure we'll all enjoy it. But first, let's head down to the office where our team has been patiently waiting."

Chapter Twelve

K IT HAD SAT through the entire meeting with the Wolf brothers' pack members and marveled at the scope of their member's infiltration into the upper echelons of the city's government and business organizations. She watched as the men discussed her as if she wasn't even present and despite being impressed with their company, she was starting to get mighty tired of being treated as if she was invisible. She had a glass of water in her hand, and when she looked down, she noticed it was bubbling.

She hadn't even realized Trev was speaking to her until he knelt down in front of her. "Kit, can you hear me?" She heard the genuine concern in his voice and as much as she wanted to assure him that she was fine, the truth was she wasn't sure. "Kit, look at me, baby." She didn't even realize she'd returned her gaze to the glass; even though the bubbles had stopped she was still stunned by what had happened.

Just as she brought her eyes up to meet Trev's again she heard the sound of chimes and wondered if maybe that old expression "Saved by the bell" might be more truth than myth. Well, that *is* she wondered until she heard her mother's voice in the hall. Groaning, she just shook her head and then whispered, "I'm so sorry. No one deserves what you are about to be subjected to." And before Kit had even taken her next breath, Carla Harris swept into the room.

JAMESON GAVE THEIR sweet housekeeper a small smile when she seemed totally flustered by the audacity of the woman who had obviously simply ignored her attempts to corral her in the entryway. Instead, the tornado had just swept into their office unannounced. There wasn't any question, the radiant woman was Kit's mother. The resemblance was undeniable. He'd bet the polished looking man following in Kit's mother's footsteps was her father. The smaller and much older woman with the mischievous glint in her eyes was probably the grandmother Kit mentioned. When the woman realized she'd stormed in to a meeting, she didn't appear to be the least bit fazed. "Nice to meet you, gentlemen. I'm Carla Harris and this is my husband Richard. And that ornery old woman behind me is my mother, Ruby."

Jameson about lost it when he nodded at the older woman, she grinned and pulled her long skirt up enough to reveal sparkling red high top Reeboks.

"Oh there you are Kathleen, mercy you have been awfully hard to tract down, dear. And we've been so worried."

Jameson was sure he'd seen Kit mouth the word "sorry" to Trev when she'd heard her mother's voice in the hall, but he hadn't been able to make out the rest of what she'd said.

When Carla reached Kit she'd grabbed the glass, stuck her finger in the water, and then laughed. "Perfect! Did it bubble?" When Kit slowly nodded, Carla clapped her hands together gleefully. Then pointing to Trev, she asked, "This one?" When Jameson saw his sweet kitten drop her face into her hands he decided he'd stood back and let Carla Harris rule his office long enough.

Stepping forward Jameson deliberately approached Richard Harris first, "Hello, Richard Harris, Kit's father, I assume? I'm Jameson Wolf and the man kneeling before Kit is my brother, Trevlon. Welcome to our home and specifically Trev's and my office. We were just having a strategy meeting with our security staff so we can ensure Kit's safety. Any additional information you can provide will be appreciated."

Jameson could see the stunned expression on the man's face. No doubt he was accustomed to being overlooked as people dealt with his much more Alpha wife and Jameson had to admit, the woman radiated magical power. He also noticed Ruby's sly wink and smile of approval. She knew exactly what Jameson had done and why. And if he wasn't mistaken, he'd just made a new friend.

Richard Harris shook his hand and Jameson didn't miss the small smile on his lips. He thanked Jameson for his hospitality and explained they'd been trying to track their daughter with a couple of tokens in her purse but that with all the electronic security equipment in the Wolf's estate house, it hadn't been as simple as it should have been. Looking over at Kit with obvious affection, he asked, "Kit darling, are you alright? We've been so worried about you." The man's sincere concern for his daughter warmed Jameson's heart and he could see Trev was equally impressed.

Watching Kit move into her father's outstretched arms touched Jameson's heart. Richard was tall, but not imposing and his lean physique was a testament to his shifter heritage. His dark hair and eyes gave him a look that might have seemed intimidating, but his entire demeanor radiated a peaceful countenance. Turning to Carla, he said, "It's nice to meet you Mrs. Harris and while I wish it was under more pleasant circumstances, we'll be happy to hear anything you have to add as well." He saw recognition in her eyes a second before she masked it, but in that second he'd gotten his answer. This woman was indeed the woman who had tried to save his parents and he made a silent pledge to cut her some slack and keep focused on the fact that his goal was to make sure her daughter was safe and happy. He and Trev would make it their life's mission to make sure Kit's life was as perfect as possible and that her parents never again had to worry about whether or not she was in danger.

Jameson and Trev worked together to get everyone settled back down and re-focused on the topic at hand—keeping Kit safe. After they had seated everyone, Carla turned to face both he and Trev before speaking, "As I'm sure you have noticed there is a very strong bond between you and Kathleen and I'm sure you have chalked it up to the typical mating attraction, but let me assure you it is much more than that."

Not being a big fan of dramatic presentations in general, and particularly not when he felt someone was dangling information just out of his reach, Jameson pressed, "Could you please explain that statement, Mrs. Harris? Because I have to tell you, I'm anxious to get this meeting taken care of because as I'm looking on, my mate is visibly wilting. Kit is tired and overwhelmed, and at this moment I don't feel like my brother and I are doing a very good job of caring for her. So...no disrespect intended, but cut to the chase, please."

This time there was no mistaking the smile that spread

over Ruby's lips, nor did Jameson miss the slight lowering of her head in deference to his Alpha status. He returned her nod as an acknowledgement and then returned his attention to Carla Harris who obviously had not missed his interaction with her mother. While it was easy to see the two women were related, it was equally clear they dealt with people in entirely different manners. Ruby appeared to watch and assess while Carla seemed the type to run headlong into the roar.

Carla seemed to glance around the room and note there were quite a few people in attendance before speaking again. "Without going in to a lot of detail, I'll say this *mating* was predestined and has been highly anticipated in both magical and shifter circles." She took a deep breath and then for the first time he saw a hint of compassion in her eyes. "That is not to say everyone is thrilled that it has finally happened. You see, while it was common knowledge in those circles that a powerful merging between a child with great magical ability and a very dominant pack leader was predicted, only a very few people knew the specifics. The prophecy speaks to the upsurge of good that will follow and anytime one side is able to tip the delicate balance of power in their favor the other side is going to fight it with everything they have. Some of the fight took place a long time ago…it was a pre-emptive strike so to speak. Damian is one of the dark side's leaders and he has been taken a very personal interest in the three of you. He failed in his attempt that night and he didn't take it well." Carla's rueful smile told Jameson she had deliberately understated this Damian character's reaction. And if he didn't miss his guess it wasn't something she did often.

Trev's words blasted into his mind, '*Oh my fucking God.*

Carla Harris was there that night to help our parents defend us, not to defend our parents.' Jameson wasn't surprised that his twin had processed the information at the speed of light, but he wasn't completely convinced yet. It was almost incomprehensible to Jameson that this could have escaped them for all of these years. He didn't answer his brother, mostly because he was just too overwhelmed at the thought that all three of their parents had died that night defending them. They had always believed the attack was directed at their sweet mother because of her magical abilities, but it had never made that much sense either. She had drawn symbols of protection on each of them and then locked them safely away when they could have easily been a lot of help.

Carla seemed to sense the fact he and Trev were scrambling to process everything she'd said, as well as what she'd left unspoken because her voice was filled with compassion when she spoke again. "Jameson, Trevlon…I know this is overwhelming and hard for you to consider because this is not at all the way you have remembered that night. But please believe me, your parents made the sacrifice with nothing but love in their hearts. They knew exactly what they were doing and I swear to you, we all fought with everything we had."

And there it was—the confirmation that she had been the witch who had joined the fight that night. Unfortunately it seemed to raise more questions than it answered. And right now he needed to focus on keeping Kit safe because things had just gotten a whole lot more complicated.

Chapter Thirteen

KIT WAS SURE there had to be at least one other conversation taking place in the room aside from what her mom was sharing because the air between Trev and Jameson was practically crackling. There had been several times she felt they were communicating telepathically and this looked like it was definitely one of those moments. Then, there were her mother's strange words. Kit listened but she was having trouble tracking everything that was taking place in the room and her fingers felt like they were almost tingling. *What the hell is that about?* Wait, what did my mom just say? *Damn it, Kit, focus for God's sake.* It was as if she knew her men's parents. *Her men?* Oh Lord, where had that thought come from? *Yes indeed Alice...you have fallen through that damned looking glass again.*

Listening as her mother described the details of the night Jameson and Trev's parents were killed was like listening as someone described one of the seven levels of hell. Kit remembered how terribly injured her mother had been when her grandmother had finally brought her back to their home. She also remembered how frustrated her father had been with both his wife and mother-in-law for not sharing more details of the "incident" with them.

As she recalled, her dad had drawn a line in the sand after that incident. He'd told her mother that she needed to consider her obligations to her own family as well as those she felt for the magical community. Kit had been helping her grandmother clean her mother's wounds when he'd spoken the words and she remembered her mother's response had surprised her. Her mom had locked her gaze on Kit as she'd whispered, "Richard, it *was* for Kathleen, it was *all* for her."

Suddenly the room was spinning and Kit felt like she couldn't catch her breath, even though she could hear herself gasping it didn't seem like any of the oxygen was actually making it into her lungs. And there was that damned tingling in her fingers again. When had it gotten so hot in this room? And if someone would just make things stop spinning maybe she could get up and go outside. When she tried to stand everything seemed to tip to the left just before darkness closed in on her from all directions swamping her.

TREV HAD FELT the anxiety coming off Kit in waves and had called her name several times without getting a response. When she tried to get to her feet, he knew she was in trouble because her breathing was so fast and shallow he was sure she must be feeling as if she wasn't getting any air at all. Then when her eyes had rolled back a split second before she collapsed he was grateful he'd already started picking her up. She'd been muttering something about "her men" but Trev hadn't been able to make it out.

When her entire body went lax in his arms he curled her further into his chest and started making his way out of the room. "Jameson, please make sure Kit's family is comfortable and then come on upstairs as quickly as possible. We need to take care of our mate. Tristan and our security team can handle things for a while."

Trev wasn't that surprised when Kit's grandmother stepped out of the door behind him. When she touched his arm, he felt an arc of electricity and somehow knew in that instant she had read him like a book. He was relieved at her warm smile. She stood on her tiptoes and leaned over to brush a soft kiss over Kit's forehead. "She is so beautiful...inside and out. She always has been. She and her grandfather were so very close and I know she has missed him terribly. I'm so glad she has you and your brother now. But make no mistake, Trevlon, she is in great danger. Your mating will fulfill a prophecy that many fear."

There were a hundred questions going through his mind and Trev knew this woman would likely give him much more honest and straightforward answers than he or Jameson would get from her daughter, but this wasn't the time for the discussion. "Ruby, my brother and I thank you for coming, and we'll both enjoy speaking with you as soon as we have some time with Kit. Her safety is our first priority and that also includes making sure she is well cared for." Smiling into her age-worn face, Trev saw a flash of sadness that spoke volumes about how much she obviously missed her recently deceased husband. The misty memory lingered in her eyes just a moment before he was once again warmed by her smile.

"By all means, please," she spoke softly as she stepped aside and gestured for him to proceed.

He nodded and started to step away, but stopped and leaned down and kissed her deeply lined forehead and whispered, "It's very easy to see why Kit is so special. She obviously has had some wonderful role models. We'll speak again soon. Please let our pack members make you comfortable in our home."

Making his way down the hall, he felt Kit's fingers stroking his chin. When he looked down into her emerald eyes, he smiled at her and felt her soul linking itself even stronger to his own. If he hadn't been a shifter, he might have missed her softly spoken words, "Thank you." He'd always considered their enhanced hearing an advantage, but not until Kit, had he understood the true depth of the gift. Being able to make out her sweet words would always fill a special part of his heart.

Trev didn't know exactly what she was thanking him for, so he just smiled and said "You are welcome, baby." He suspected it was for the kindness he'd shown her grandmother. But in truth it didn't matter, if she was happy, that was all that concerned him. She didn't know it yet, but she would soon—there wasn't anything he and his brother wouldn't do for her. He didn't care about a prophecy. Right now he wasn't interested in anything but this moment and the woman nestled securely in his arms.

Entering their suite, Trev was pleased to see the housekeepers they employed had already been in and had left everything in pristine order. Employing the younger members of the pack was a tradition their fathers had started, and Jameson and Trev had been happy to continue. It not only allowed the young people to learn the value of a good work ethic and money management, but it also allowed the pack Alphas opportunities to get to know their members individually. Their fathers had always said it was easier to mentor and lead people you actually *knew*.

Setting Kit gently on her feet near the sofa, he brushed the backs of his fingers over her cheek and just looked at her for long seconds. He'd been stunned by her beauty the first moment he'd seen her, and even though he'd been physically drawn to many women over the years, it pleased him the attraction he felt for Kit seemed to be growing not weakening. "Baby, I'm sorry we didn't shut that down sooner. Jameson and I should have sensed your distress earlier, and I apologize that we let it get so far gone."

The puzzled look on her face told him she didn't yet understand the depth of what *matings* meant and he wasn't sure exactly how to explain it. He had always been better with actions—while words were more Jameson's strong suit. "Baby, as your mates it will be our job to take care of you and that means a lot of things to us. One of those is seeing to your emotional well-being. We should have detected how stressed you were and intervened on your behalf."

KIT FELT LIKE her brain was finally starting to fire on most of its cylinders again, because she couldn't decide whether to be outraged at his audacity or touched by his sentiment. "But...it's my job to make sure I'm okay. I am an adult and have been taking care of myself for a very long time, Trev. I don't need a *keeper*...well, not most of the time anyway." She tried to take some of the sting out of her words because she didn't want to hurt his feelings and she had a suspicion that was exactly where she'd been headed.

"I'm not trying to be ungrateful, Trev, but I want you to know that what happened downstairs was in no way your fault. And well, you see...oh my, I should wait until Jameson is here to speak of this." Just as she'd spoken the words the door of the bedroom burst open. Kit turned, expecting to see Jameson, but was nearly steamrolled by Libby.

"Holy fucking shit. Did you know your parents are

here and your grandmother, too? She's a kick, by the way, and she promised to get me a pair of those sneakers. And they said your apartment blew up, did you know that? Geez, are your parents in the mafia or something because no offense, but your mother has a major stick up her ass. And your dad has this suave, silent but deadly gentlemen thing going that is to die for. I'll bet he was a hottie in his day." Libby was in fine form and her brilliant blue eyes were practically dancing. Kit couldn't help but laugh because everything she had just spit out in her five-second outburst had been on-point. People tended to grossly underestimate Libby because of her appearance. Just the fact she was tiny and blonde, people tended to assume she was a stereotypical blonde when nothing could be further from the truth.

Libby Wells, only thirty-two years old, was already a fully tenured professor at NYU with PhDs in both chemistry and neuroscience. She had published so many articles that Kit's eyes had glazed over looking at the framed copies of the covers from various professional journals on the wall in her office one afternoon. The woman was positively brilliant and her mind *and* her mouth both moved at the speed of light.

Kit had met Libby her first day of teaching Romantic Literature at the university and despite their hugely divergent areas of interest, they'd become fast friends. "Well as usual my friend, you have nailed each of those people dead center. You're remarkable at that by the way, just in case I haven't mentioned it a thousand and one times." She grinned at her friend and then continued, "I did hear about my apartment, but my main concern has been Dusty. But I got a message from his mom a bit ago and she assures me he is fine and looking forward to our next park play date so I'll just have to trust that for now. And there seems to be some reason to believe I might be in danger, so I'll be staying here for this week. And thank you in advance for bringing me so many things and my laptop because as of now those are my sole possessions."

She'd tried to smile as she said the words, but her eyes had filled with tears all on their own. Libby had taken one look at her and quickly stepped forward to wrap her arms around her. "Oh, girlfriend, it'll be okay. Damn, I'm not saying it doesn't suck, because it sucks big green donkey dicks actually, but you're safe here." She pulled Kit down to whisper in her ear, "And spending the week with those two hunks that are hovering around you like they plan to devour you can't be a real hardship."

Wiping her tears, Kit thanked Libby yet again before Charlie escorted her from the room. The young man had smiled over his shoulder at his bosses and then just shook his head as if he didn't have any real idea how to deal with the pint-sized dynamo. *Welcome to NYU's world, Charlie.*

Chapter Fourteen

J AMESON HAD WATCHED the interaction between Kit and her friend and it had taken every ounce of self-control he'd been able to muster to keep from pulling her into his own arms when he'd seen her beautiful green eyes swimming in tears. He was glad he'd waited because the women seemed to have had a calming effect on each other and he knew how important friendship was, even though his twin had always fulfilled that role in his own life.

"Kitten, come here." Jameson stood just a few feet from Kit, but he was going to start subtly introducing her to the ways of pack life as well as their expectations as her mates and Doms. She only hesitated for the briefest of seconds before she closed the gap between them. Her slender feet were still bare and the bubble-gum pink polish on her tiny toes was going to be the death of his control. When she was standing so close, he could feel her body's heat searing into his lower abdomen he ran his fingers through her hair and just studied her for long seconds. "Are you alright, my love?"

"Yes, I'm fine, really. It's just been, well…it's been kind of a challenging end of the week. And I seem to be battling things on several fronts and…" Jameson could feel the frustration radiating off her and he appreciated that she hadn't tried to lie to him. "Well, you know, there are so many things to think about and hearing all of that stuff my mom was saying and putting that together with what I remember about the night and then there is this crazy thing between us." He saw her take a couple of deep breaths and he was determined to wait her out. He knew she hadn't finished what she started to say and he wanted her to get it off her chest.

"You guys know so much more about how this works and I was interested in learning, and sex with you is so amazing, but now it seems like we don't really have any options. Honestly, I don't want you to be with me because you have to fulfill some damned prophecy. Geez, you might have gotten to know me and decided I was just too much of a 'Do it yourself, handy-man special' you know? And maybe you didn't want a woman with so much baggage and that some little furry piece of fluff without a crazy-assed witch—literally—for a mother would be a lot easier to deal with."

This time when she stopped talking Jameson decided he'd let it go on long enough. He smiled down at her, "Kitten, I want you to know I'm very proud of you and your honesty is a testament to the fact Trev and I have already started building a level of trust among the three of us and that is exactly as we want it to be. Now, I should address each of those points individually—especially those pertaining to you being someone we'd feel a need to *fix,* but quite frankly, I'm not sure I'd get through that particular point without paddling your sweet ass. So, let's just cut to the chase and say we would never mate with someone just because we were told it fulfilled some sort of prophecy. No, sweet kitten, you were ours the minute I started down the stairs at the club and knew my brother's and my mate was in the room. Walking up behind you as you stood at the bar and then seeing into your soul when you turned into my chest was a defining point in my life I will never forget."

Trev had stepped up behind Kit and was rubbing his hands lightly up and down her slender arms. They'd dressed her in a next to nothing dress to take her downstairs because they had planned to keep their hands on her the entire time and didn't want anything to keep them from touching her bare skin. However, when things had gone from sugar to shit he had wished she'd had on something she would have felt more confident in. Jameson saw Trev lean down and then heard him whisper, "Baby, you are so amazing. I know you don't understand how perfect you are, but my brother and I will be happy to spend the rest of our lives proving it to you each and every day."

Jameson placed his finger over her lips when she started to speak. "Kitten, if you are getting ready to disagree with anything my brother just said, let me caution you that remarks that take aim at the incredible person you are will be dealt with quickly and harshly. Do you understand?" He knew he was pushing her, but he also knew Kit was an extremely bright woman who had already admitted an interest in their lifestyle, so he wasn't as worried as he might have been with someone who hadn't ever given Dominance and submission any consideration.

When Kit nodded her head, Jameson continued, "Now, do you still want to say what you started to say earlier? Or would you like to reconsider your words?"

He didn't even try to hide his smile when she just shook her head no and quietly conceded, "I think I should probably reconsider. I'm sorry, I'm just a bit overwhelmed and horny and well...that is probably not the best combination of emotions for making decisions."

Jameson smiled, "I'm betting that was awfully hard for you to admit because I can see how much your independence means to you. So before we go any further I want you to know, Trev and I have no intention of taking away anything that you value. Now, that doesn't mean we'll be willing to stand idly by and let someone hurt you. Nor will be willing to stand aside and let you put yourself in danger—physical *or* emotional danger, kitten. We won't distinguish between types of danger and our reactions will be quick and decisive. It's important you know that. We are protective and possessive, and you are *ours*."

When he'd finished talking he crashed his mouth over hers. He'd decided the time for words had passed and it was now time to show her exactly how they felt. The hot, smooth texture of her satiny lips sliding against his was enough to make him moan his need into her mouth. It was as if that small infusion of sound lit a fire inside of his sweet mate because she seemed to come to life in that instant. Kit was trying to crawl up him as if he were a tree and she was seeking the sweetest, ripest fruit that she believed was hiding at the top.

Coming up for air was a necessary, but unwanted separation. Jameson took just enough time to draw in much needed oxygen before moving his mouth back down to caress the pulse point at the side of Kit's slender neck. "Your pulse is racing, kitten. Tell me what your body is saying to you. Listen with your heart, not that brilliant mind Trev and I admire so much. Do you want us as much as we want you?" Jameson could hear the gruffness in his voice, the barely leashed need to claim and conquer.

"I want you more than I even know words to explain. You both set everything in me on fire, yet I'm terrified of the claiming. I have never wanted to *belong* to anyone before so the depth of the desire I feel now is frightening." Again Jameson was caught off guard by the crystal clear honesty of Kit's answer. Dealing with women who frequented their club throughout the years had obviously left him more jaded than he'd known because honesty should have been his expectation with his mate, but it wasn't.

Trev had never stopped touching Kit and even though they weren't actually speaking through their mind-link, Jameson was able to tap into his twin's emotions and could feel the love he had for Kit racing through his heart and mind just as it was his own. Trev leaned even closer as he spoke, "Baby, claiming is going to bring about changes for you that it doesn't for most mates, so we understand your hesitance. But we want you to know there has never been a day that you haven't belonged to us. Just because we hadn't yet found you, doesn't mean we didn't already love you. We have been searching for you for a very long time."

When Trev's voice pushed into Jameson's mind, gone was the passion-fueled timber of a lover. In place was the beast pushing to bite and claim. *'I have to run tonight or I'm going to claim her with or without her consent and I don't want to do that. I haven't run since we met her and the coming full moon is pressing down upon me like a ton of rock.'*

As much as Jameson would have liked to answer, he could only manage a quick, barely noticeable nod because he was facing a similar problem himself. He'd already decided they would run tonight. He made arrangements for some of their female pack members to spend the evening with Kit and he figured that would serve two purposes. The males would get to run and the women would have a chance to answer Kit's questions.

Turning his attention back to Kit, he asked her, "Are you wet for us, kitten?"

She seemed surprised by his change of pace but he immediately smelled another wash of her arousal as her body responded to his question by preparing itself once again for her mates. When she didn't answer him, he moved his hands to her distended nipples and pinched them just hard enough that he knew she would feel the electric spike of pain just before she realized her body was changing the pain to pleasure in a way her mind couldn't yet process. Her loud moan was his cue to press the issue, "Kitten, I asked you a question. We will always expect you to answer with words when we ask you a question, do you understand?"

"Oh, yes, I understand. But it felt so…I don't even know how to describe it. But yes, I am so very wet for you. It's like my body and my mind are working independently when I am near you."

Trev leaned over her shoulder and licked a line along her collarbone before moving his mouth back to her shoulder. "Every cell in your body is pushing your mating scent out so it calls to us in a way we can barely resist. Let us show you how it feels to hold the attention of two men in your body at the same time." Jameson felt Kit's body tense and he was sure Trev wouldn't have missed it either. "We'll go as slow as you need to, baby, but I can promise you that by the time we get to that point, you'll be begging us to take you together. Are you brave enough to go after the pleasure that can be yours, sweetness?"

Jameson had to hide his smile because it was obvious their mate wasn't one to let a challenge pass by without responding and she didn't disappoint him.

"I'd like very much to find out if I can meet that challenge, Trev. But at the same time…it frightens me. And just for the record, I know what you have done." The smile on her face let him know that she'd understood the purpose of the challenge, but the fact her smile didn't quite reach her eyes reminded him that her fear was real.

"Understandable. Do you trust us to keep you safe? You've seen how a bite of pain can morph into pure pleasure. Are you willing to push yourself to get there?" Trev had always claimed it was Jameson who could use words alone to bring a woman to the peak, but his opinion, Trev was doing a mighty fine job of walking Kit up that mountain himself so he held his own words. It seemed that a challenge was what it was going to take to get Kit to push herself even though she'd called Trev out on it. They all knew this was a natural progression in any ménage relationship and the pleasure was going to be mind-blowing. The only question was whether or not Kit was ready and Jameson found himself holding his breath waiting for her to answer.

CHAPTER FIFTEEN

T REV KNEW HE was pushing Kit, but he also knew she was ready. Jameson was the stricter of the two of them, but Trev had always been the edgier of them. And Trev was sure he was reading her signals accurately. Her body was broadcasting her need as clearly as if she had shouted it from the rooftop. She let her head fall back onto his shoulder and groaned softly when Jameson sucked a nipple into his mouth and he pinched the other one. Trev barely heard her whispered words, "Oh God, please...show me."

"Those were the sweetest words I've ever heard, baby. And they sounded more like a prayer than demand so we're going to reward you with the more pleasure than even your imagination thinks you can experience." They had already started making their way toward the bed and he wasn't sure she was even aware of the fact they were moving. Pulling his fingers through the soft, wet folds of her pussy and watching as her hips thrust involuntarily into his touch was enough to make him want to sink fast and deep, and worry about slow and easy next time. He knew this was going to be a torturous exercise in self-control, but the reward was going to be heaven. Trev took a steadying breath and tried to focus every bit of his attention on each and every nuance of Kit's reactions.

Turning Kit in his arms so he could devour her sweet

mouth with his own while Jameson turned down the bed and got into position, Trev used his tongue to mimic what their cocks were going to be doing to her pretty pink pussy and tight little ass in just a few short minutes. When he felt the air around him start to crackle he knew she was getting close to release. Pulling from her lips, he moved just enough to the side to get his hand between them and turned his palm so it cupped her sex and felt her breath hitch. Then she moaned, "Please let me come, I need to come." The sound went straight to his cock.

"We want your channel flooded and relaxed when we take you together, baby. This is going to be a night we will all remember for the rest of our lives. Crawl up on the bed and lower that sweet cunt of yours over your Alpha's cock. He's waiting for you, baby." He heard her startled gasp at his crude words, but he also felt her shiver as her arousal washed over his fingers. Hell, she was so fucking wet it was literally dripping on the floor. Trev couldn't wait until they took her in the meadow under the full moon. Seeing her delectable body in her wolf with her ass peaked in front of them as she lowered her front shoulders to the ground was going to a moment he was sure would burn itself permanently into his memory.

JAMESON WATCHED AS Trev helped Kit get up on the bed and handed her into his care. Then Trev just stepped back and Jameson knew his twin was no doubt enjoying the view of Kit's bare ass and pussy as she crawled closer when he'd beckoned her. "Come here, kitten. I want to slide deep into you and feel all that wet, searing heat surround my cock. I want to lean back and watch as your luscious breasts move with increasing fervor as you ride me. Your peach-colored nipples are already peaked and darkening to that dusty rose we love so much, kitten. Are you wet for me as well?"

Kit's breath hitched and Jameson saw her chest rising in time with her short panting breaths. Watching the flush of arousal paint her body in a soft pink was the most erotic thing he'd ever seen. "That's it, kitten. Now lower your hot sheath over my cock. Oh my fucking God." Jameson was going to lose his mind at this rate, the feel of her muscles flexing around him as her body worked to take him to the root was going to pull the seed from his balls long before he was ready if he didn't find a way to distract himself. When he was finally able to focus his eyes on something other than where his body was sinking into hers, he looked up into her gaze and felt like he'd been gut-punched at the look of undiluted lust he saw dancing in her eyes.

"You are doing beautifully, kitten. And I can't begin to tell you how close you are to making me come. Hell, I could come just from watching your eyes as the pleasure writes itself in your expression." Jameson let her fuck herself on his cock for several minutes. The pleasure was almost blinding in its intensity. When he knew she was close to her release, he reached forward and squeezed her clit between his fingers just as he commanded her release. "Come for me, mate."

Watching as Kit threw her head back and screamed his name was a sight to behold. The look of pure rapture was intoxicating and the feel of her hot sex gripping him like a fist was exquisite. And he had barely been able to contain his joy as he watched the sparkles that seemed to dance over her skin as if someone had lit her from within with a thousand tiny sparklers. Pulling her down against his chest, he spoke against her ear, "That was amazing. Watching you lose yourself in pleasure is spell-binding, kitten."

Jameson didn't have to see Trev to know he had moved into position behind Kit because he felt her tense in response. "We're going to take this really slow, my love. Let Trev prepare you. His fingers are going to work some very special magic if you'll just follow his lead."

"You are so hot, baby. Talk to me. Tell me how it feels, Kit." Trev's voice was already roughened and Jameson knew his brother was struggling to keep things at a slow pace. Kit would be able to deal with their size as long as she was properly prepared. The key was to keep a tight hold on her so once Trev did start to impale her she didn't lose herself in desire and push back too soon.

"It feels so strange…it burns, but it feels so good at the same time. I…well, I don't know how that can be, but it is….oh dear God." Jameson glanced up at Trev and saw the satisfaction in his brother's eyes and he had to wonder what Trev had done to provoke her outburst.

"Come on baby, stay with me here. What were you saying?" There was humor in Trev's tone that Jameson was sure would be lost on Kit because she was quickly falling over the edge of submission. Jameson tightened his hold on her as he felt her begin to rock back and forth. "Hold her, brother." Jameson banded his arms around her and began caressing the shell of her ear with his tongue just as he felt her jolt in his arms.

"Oh my sweet kitten, tell me what my brother is doing to you."

"His fingers…they are inside my ass and they are…opening and turning in circles and if he doesn't hurry I'm going to go out of my mind," Kit's voice was airy and lacked its usual cool distance.

"Are you ready for me, baby?" Trev's words were spoken just before he heard Kit's gasp and he could literally hear her blood rushing through her veins. And the feel of her heart beating wildly in her chest where it was pressed tight against his own sent even more blood to his throbbing cock. *'Christ I'm going to die of pleasure beneath our mate before we're both inside her.'*

KIT WASN'T GOING to survive the next thirty seconds, she was absolutely sure of it. She couldn't even think because every inch of her body felt like it was being consumed by a fire burning its way from her core up to the flaming surface of her tingling skin. And being able to tighten her internal muscles and feel the veins and ridges of Jameson's cock inside her was sweet torture. When she tightened on him, he let out the most delightful little moans as if she was the one torturing him. Jameson's warm breath against her ear, the kisses and nibbles to its sensitive shell were making her crazy and each time she even thought about pushing back against Trev, Jameson seemed to sense it and tighten the steel bands he called arms around her until she was straining just to take a deep breath. "Please...please I need more." She knew she was begging exactly as Trev had said she would but at this point, she really didn't care.

When she felt Trev remove his fingers from her ass she moaned at the loss. "Oh, baby, I'm going to give you more. I'm going to give you so much more you won't know where you end and I begin. Are you ready for me?" Kit thought he was going to rip her in two when the tip of his cock started to breach the sensitive muscles encircling her anus. But then just as she thought she couldn't take any more, the pain began to morph into the most incredible, wicked pleasure she could have ever imagined. "Tell me what just went through your head, baby. Tell me now, Kit. Your whole body shifted and the sound you made in the back of your throat was from your wolf. *Now, Kit.*"

His words were demanding, but exactly what she needed to bring herself back. For the first time she had actually "felt" her inner wolf clawing to be set free and in another second she would have begged them to bite her...to claim her. Even though it seemed that it was probably a foregone conclusion, she'd like to have a bit more of their "wooing" before they got to the sinking teeth into her body part. She managed to suppress her shudder, but just barely.

She suddenly realized that neither Jameson nor Trev were moving. It took her several more seconds to realize they were still waiting for her answer. Now if she could just pull her head out of her ass long enough to remember what Trev had asked her. "I'm sorry...could you ask your question again, please? I sort of...well, I sort of got distracted by all the sensations crashing into me from every direction and I couldn't seem to stay in the moment."

"I asked you what had gone through your head, baby. And I want an answer right now. And don't you dare lie or edit because I will know and I'll light your sweet ass up with a single-tail if you even think about trying to deceive us on this." Kit heard the growl in his voice and had to smile because the one thing she was well known for was being honest...usually much too honest for most people's comfort.

"The pain...I couldn't help but wonder why it changes." As soon as she had started speaking, Trev and Jameson had gone back to caressing her with the lightest of touches and it was sending chill bumps racing over every square inch of her body. "Oh God, please...I need..." Her words were cut off by a moan that came from the back of her throat when Trev started to slowly pull from her rear hole.

"We know exactly what you need Kit. And we'll give it to you, I promise. But you need to finish answering Trev's question or we'll show you exactly how long we can keep you dancing on this edge and how long we can deny your orgasm if we want to. Now, tell us about how the pain changed or Trev is going to use a single tail on this beautiful ivory ass and I don't think you are ready for that just yet."

Just yet? Is he fucking kidding? "Just as the pain seemed to be...well, like it was too much. Just the instant before I was going to tell you I was ready to quit, it started to change into...oh God, when you do that I can barely remember my own name, let alone form a coherent sentence or finish a thought about something I don't really understand." She tried to thrust back against Trev, but once again Jameson seemed to have read her thoughts and tightened his hold just before she'd made the move.

"Oh no you don't, my lovely mate, this is our show and you are going to hurt yourself if you don't let us stretch that beautiful ass hole of yours nice and slow. Now, keep talking, kitten." She heard the Dominance in his voice and recognized its power as an Alpha immediately. She'd read about the compelling voices of pack Alphas, but had never had any personal experience with it until this moment.

"The pain is almost an exquisite rush of heat that reminds me of molten lava rolling down the sides of the mountain. When the liquid fire reaches the sea it sizzles and is instantly changed into solid rock. And this pain reminds me of that as it crosses the line from hurting in a bad way to hurting in a good way just by your cool touch. I don't understand exactly how that works, but...Oh my fucking Lord of the Lamps." As soon as they'd started stroking her in alternating thrust and retreat motions she had lost every reasonable thought. It was like having every cell in your body touched by an electrical current at the exact same moment. There was no way she could have spoken another word.

There must have been something in her response to their question that they both liked because they had begun working in tandem without so much as a heartbeat between their motions. As Trev withdrew his velvet covered steel from her ass Jameson was sinking his inside her pussy and she could feel the swollen mushroom-shaped head pressing inside her so deep she wondered if he could feel the end of her channel.

She watched in wonder as Jameson's eyes narrowed and sparks of gold started to flicker in their depths lighting up the color like a million amber leaves flickering in a crisp fall breeze. And then as if he'd actually heard her thoughts, he spoke in a voice that sounded like it had been polished with sand paper, "The head of my cock is pressing against your cervix, do you like that, kitten?" When she moaned her assent, his growl was unmistakable.

Kit felt Jameson's attention shift to his brother and then as if they'd spoken again through what they'd explained as their "twin bond". They had mentioned the three of them would be able to speak telepathically once they were mated and she wondered how the process worked. Was the communication actually conversational? Could they block it if they wanted to? Would her thoughts...all of them be open to them after they were mated? The questions were racing through her mind at the speed of light but they felt like they were being fired in a random pattern. She couldn't seem to track a thought for longer than a few seconds, and that was probably an optimistic estimate.

"We'll answer each of those questions—later, my love. But right now, we want every bit of your attention right here, right between us. We want your heart and mind centered on the pleasure of being filled with the cocks of both your mates. Keep yourself—right here—right *now*. Come for us, kitten." Kit knew her body had reacted to Jameson's words a heartbeat before her mind had even understood his words. She felt as if she'd been launched over the edge of a deep ravine...rapid acceleration and then the sweet floating of a free-fall.

She heard a scream and it wasn't until she was gasping for her breath that she realized she'd been the one screaming both Jameson and Trev's names as her mind had exploded in splintering shards of pure pleasure. At the moment her orgasm had peaked, she'd heard both men growl their own releases and she had felt herself being filled with their seed. It was as if she were melting from the inside out and she collapsed in a flattened remnant of her former self atop Jameson's chest and listened as his heart thundered under her ear. Kit closed her eyes in satisfaction when he hugged her tightly and let her mind savor the joy of being sheltered. She knew that everything she had believed about herself...every dream she'd always believed to be important was coming completely apart...molecule by molecule and floating away, and she was just too exhausted to fight it.

CHAPTER SIXTEEN

*A*FTER THEY'D CLEANED Kit carefully and tucked her into bed for a short nap, Jameson and Trev had stationed two of their most trusted security staff just outside the door before they made their way down the back stairs. They had decided a short run this evening would have to do because neither of them had any desire to be away from their future mate for very long. They would be able to catch up on a few calls in their office while a few of the women entertained Kit later this evening. Jameson knew the women were looking forward to meeting her and he also wanted Kit to have a chance to ask the women questions as well.

The large wooden deck at the back of the house was bathed in the first rays of moonlight and the depth of the shadows gave the entire area an almost eerie appearance. They usually ran much later at night because there was less chance of running into their neighbors, but tonight they were going to be staying close enough to home it wouldn't matter. Just as they stepped outside, Jameson looked at Trev and shook his head. "Did you see the candles in our room light on their own when she came? It was the most amazing thing I've ever seen."

Trev laughed, "I did and I'm glad those candles were there, hell who knows what might have spontaneously burst into flames if they hadn't been nearby. God, she is amazing." Because they had recently hosted several events for charity, there had been so many people in and out of their compound, so neither of them noticed the man standing in the shadows of the nearby trees listening to their every word. Shifters enhanced senses weren't without their limits and it was easy for Damian to mask his scent. Dark magic had always blurred the lines between what nature had intended and what evil craved. He had been battling for years to break through the seal the three witches had placed over the portal and the fact he'd only been able to kill one of them and had failed to kill her sons still shamed him.

Jameson stepped out of his gym shorts and tossed them aside. "Let's get changed and run. I want to get back to Kit. The hair is standing up on the back of my neck and I don't want to leave her unattended for long." His words were immediately followed by the popping of joints and the snapping of bones as they lengthened and adjusted to the men's changing forms. As their eyesight sharpened, both wolves looked around and nodded as their telepathic link took over. *'Let's run the short circle through the woods to the creek and back. I want to be back quickly so remember, this isn't a scenic tour.'*

'Yeah, I got it. Let's do this. I'm already anxious to smell our sweet woman again.' Trev had no more than let the words race through his mind than he and Jameson were both racing through the woods. They both stopped short at the edge of the trees when they scented what smelled an awful lot like the stuff local deer hunters used to mask their scent from their prey. Jameson immediately sent out a telepathic alarm to every member of the pack. He and Trev were both following the fast fading trail through the woods and the further they went away from the house the more uneasy Jameson became.

'*Who on earth would think they could mask their scent with this crap and hide from a pack of wolves? Even if we can't identify the person directly, we'd damned well know someone was trying to conceal themselves from us.*' Jameson was baffled about who would brazenly breach the perimeter of their property. Hell, they hadn't had a security challenge in several years because they made no secret of the fact their security system was state of the art. The electronic motion detectors alone usually let them know the minute anything moved through the invisible beams and their security team's response time was always less than a minute.

'*Fuck, do you suppose he's a decoy? Did you hear from the guys outside our room when you sent out the alarm?*' As soon as Trev's words registered in Jameson's mind, he knew his brother was right. They'd been deliberately drawn away from the house and it infuriated him that he'd fallen for the ruse. He immediately veered to the left and headed in a straight line back to the house with Trev fast on his heels.

'*I'm not getting any response from them. I've sent Tristen and Nick up to check, and if I know Angie, she's with them.*' Jameson was already changing as he leapt over the shrubs surrounding the large deck that ran the length of the huge main house. The original structure had been enormous, but not large enough for their rapidly expanding pack, so Jameson and Trev had added on two large wings that were each three stories tall. Their estate was home to nearly sixty people at times and even though many of those were children, they still needed rooms to sleep and play. Grabbing his gym shorts on the run and slipping them on, Jameson was a step ahead of Trev as they entered the back door. As they both ran through the door a woman's blood-chilling scream filled the air.

KIT HAD BEEN leisurely drifting in that blissful place between sleeping and fully awake when she looked up and saw a man standing just outside the window. Well, *standing* wasn't exactly accurate, because technically he was floating, but who was she to split hairs? She wasn't sure which thing had startled her most…the fact his feet weren't actually touching anything, his red glowing eyes, or the fact he was trying to speak into her mind. She knew her scream had probably been loud enough to wake the dead but she didn't care. All that mattered was getting the *thing* outside the window away from her. And then she was having a serious heart-to-heart with her mother and grandmother. It was time they answered her questions directly without their usual smoke and mirrors evasions. Kit had asked all these questions before and had gotten answers that were little more than riddles, so she'd walked away in frustration and not ever asked again. Deciding it was easier to just avoid the issues she knew mating would bring, she'd taken what she had thought was the path of least resistance and simply decided to not ever mate. Now, it appeared as though she was up against the wall and she simply no longer had any desire to participate in their usual *dance of deception.*

When her mind finally re-engaged, she realized there were people banging on the bedroom door. *Why is it locked?* She hadn't locked it and she couldn't imagine Jameson and Trev locking her in either. She knew whoever was on the other side was a split second from bursting through the door because she could hear the key sliding into the lock. Time seemed to slow to a crawl and everything seemed to be happening at the exact same moment. She saw the man outside her window looking at the door with a wand in his raised hand and she instinctively knew he was planning to hurt her mates. *My mates? When did I start thinking about them as mine?* With a flick of her wrist she sent a ball of fire crashing through the window's large pane of glass. She heard the man scream and then he simply evaporated. *Well shit, I didn't mean to do that. I just wanted to frighten him away. My mother has a lot of explaining to do, I tell you.*

She had no more than taken a deep breath than the door burst open and Jameson and Trevlon surrounded her. She hadn't even realized she had moved from the bed or that she was naked until she heard Jameson's growl and felt Trev wrap her in a blanket. When she looked up into their ferocious eyes, she wasn't afraid because their anger wasn't directed at her. All she felt was a wave of gratitude that she could now let go and relax into their arms, accepting the protection they offered, even if it was only for a few minutes.

She could see Jameson's mouth moving, but she couldn't seem to make out his words. It was as if he was speaking to her through water. Everything sounded so garbled and distant, and someone must have been dimming the lights because all of the sudden things were getting harder to see...and then everything simply went black.

CHAPTER SEVENTEEN

J AMESON HAD BEEN terrified as he'd raced up the stairs and seen several men, including Tristan and Nick, trying to get through the door to the master suite. He had no idea how the door had gotten locked—no one ever locked their doors because the cleaning crews worked such odd hours. But he knew there was a key hidden above the doorframe, which he quickly retrieved. Glancing over he saw Angie working to revive the men he'd asked to guard the door. Jameson sighed in relief when he saw them both slowly opening their eyes. But his heart had nearly stopped when he heard the sound of glass shattering inside the room just as he'd slid the key in the lock and turned the ornate doorknob. Racing across the room to where Kit stood naked in front of the now empty window frame, he was torn between gut wrenching relief that she was unharmed and blinding jealousy that Tristan and Nick were right behind them and would have seen their mate's naked body.

After Trev had wrapped Kit in a blanket she had looked at each of them, locking gazes just before her eyes seemed to roll back and then she collapsed. When Jameson had looked up, he didn't think the other men had even noticed Kit's lack of clothing because both men were staring at the bulletproof glass that had obviously been broken from the inside. How an unarmed, naked woman had managed to break glass designed to withstand machine gun fire was a mystery to him. But at this moment, he really wasn't all that interested in anything but securing Kit and making sure the rest of their pack was safe.

Trev held Kit cradled in his arms and quickly made his way over to the sitting area and settled on the large leather sofa facing the fireplace. Kit's parents and grandmother entered the room and while her father and grandmother rushed to Kit's side, her mother made her way to the window and looking outside let out a frustrated sigh, "Well, I don't know why she had to go so far overboard. We might have been able to ask *whoever that used to be* who'd sent him here." And then the inconsiderate wench had the audacity to look over at both he and his brother before adding, "Really, you two need to fuck her into submission and mate her so we can get this show on the road. I'm not getting any younger you know? And I'd like to be a grandmother before I'm too old to enjoy it. Besides, this fight is going to be a tough one, and I'm going to need her help. Mother Goddess it's cold in here."

Jameson and Trev watched as Carla Harris flipped her hand toward the large gaping hole in the wall of the master suite and instantly glass filled the window. *What the hell did she mean by* whoever that used to be? Jameson hadn't intentionally sent the thought to Trev, but he wasn't surprised when his brother picked it up.

'*No fucking clue, but she grates on my nerves. Hasn't anyone ever told her the whole world doesn't revolve around her?*' As usual, he and Trev were on exactly the same page.

"Mrs. Harris, while I appreciate you replacing the window, we'd like to attend to Kit. If you don't mind, we'd like everyone but Angie and her mates to clear the room." He saw a glimmer of a smile tip the lips of both Carla's husband and her mother before they both leaned down to kiss Kit's forehead, before moving from the room. But Carla looked at both he and Trev as if they'd just sprouted purple hair before shaking her head and then making her way out of the room.

Once everyone had moved on, Angie moved over to Kit and set her medical bag on the floor at Trev's feet. She was their cousin and at five foot seven, she was one of the tallest women in their pack. He and Trev had always been close to Angie and had teased her about being a stick figure when they had been kids. Now her willowy frame just seemed to add a sense of grace and elegance to her movements. She kept her long blonde hair tied at the base of her neck most of the time, but it was her huge chocolate brown eyes that seemed to stop everyone who met her in their tracks. Her eyes were absolutely gorgeous and they always lit up when she was plotting and scheming—which was a large portion of the time.

Angie used smelling salts to bring Kit back around. "She'll be fine, guys, don't look so worried. From what I heard from her grandmother it sounds like she used a very powerful surge of magic and she is just exhausted, but I want to be sure. I want to make sure she is alert enough to answer a few of your questions and then I want you to let her sleep it off. I'm going to wait until her parents are back in their rooms and then I'll check in with the grandmother, because I think she's going to be much more willing to give me answers. And you know, as a *medical professional* I need those answers to properly treat my patient." Angie's smile was wicked, and not for the first time Jameson thanked his lucky stars his sweet cousin was on their side.

Tristan was standing off in the corner talking in clipped tones into his phone, but Nick Michaels was standing guard over their sweet wife—well she was sweet most of the time. Nick was Tristan's younger brother but few people realized that because they were born ten months to the day apart and Nick had always looked harsher in Jameson's opinion. Nick shared Tristan's coloring and body build, but his sense of humor set him apart. Nick Michaels was always the life of the party despite his rugged appearance.

Jameson had laughed when his friends had mated with his younger cousin because he'd known she had a rebellious streak a mile wide. The brothers had claimed they would *tame* her, but as one of the lead pediatric surgeons at the Babies & Children's Hospital, which was associated with her alma mater, Columbia, Jameson and Trev had often wondered if their friends hadn't bitten off more than they could chew—literally.

Angie had graduated from high school when she was twelve and then completed medical school at twenty-two. To say she was brilliant was an understatement, but you would be hard pressed to notice unless you really listened to how insightful she was. Jameson had always felt one of Angie's greatest gifts was her ability to communicate with anyone on their own level. When their friends had started pursuing her, Angie had come to both he and Trev seeking information about their friends. The woman was a tireless researcher and she had been approaching a potential mating with the same tenacity she brought to everything else in her life. Her thirst for knowledge was matched only by her wicked sense of humor and her ferocious sense of loyalty.

Jameson sat on the sofa next to Trev, pulled Kit's legs across his lap, and gently rubbed her tiny feet more for his own comfort than for hers. He couldn't help smiling when she moaned as she came slowly awake. He listened to his brother speaking softly to their tiny mate. "Baby, can you tell us what happened?"

Jameson watched as Tristan hurriedly ended his call and made his way over so he could hear Kit's answer. "Can I please get dressed first? I'll feel better if I'm not...well, if I'm dressed with your friends in the room." Jameson was actually quite pleased with her request because as the mate of the pack's Alphas there would be expectations for her that most of the women didn't have to live up to. A certain level of decorum would be a big part of those standards.

Trev picked Kit up and moved toward the suite's bathroom, "Absolutely, baby. Jameson will bring you some clothes and then we'll all meet in the office downstairs in a bit. I'd rather we kept business out of our bedroom anyway, how's that sound?" Sounded perfect to Jameson, and as soon as he'd gotten Angie and her two mates out of the room, he'd found a pair of yoga pants and shirt for Kit and quickly made his way into the bathroom.

TREV WASN'T SURE who had been more soothed when he'd held Kit on his lap, his sweet mate or himself. Holding her in his arms and being able to feel her breathing and her heart beating reassured him that she was indeed alright. When he and Jameson had been running and realized they'd been duped his heart had squeezed in fear. They hadn't had Kit in their life long at all and already he couldn't imagine being without her. There was nothing in the world that was going to keep him from claiming Kit, but he wanted not only her consent, but he also wanted her to be happy with her decision.

When he'd heard her mother's crude words, he'd been

torn between a burning desire to do exactly as she'd said and claim Kit at that very moment and wanting to ban the woman from Kit's life. Holy Mother Goddess, Carla Harris was a pain in the ass extraordinaire. Kit's friend, Libby, had told them that Kit didn't talk about her family much, but it was obvious she tried to ignore the entire situation as much as possible because of her mother's repeated attempts to marry her off.

Helping Kit dress in the clothing Jameson had brought her was torture because he just wanted to touch and taste every inch of her rather then cover her up. But he understood how much easier their conversation would be if she had the self-confidence and *distance* that clothing would give her. He'd felt how pleased Jameson had been when she'd wanted to be dressed with the other men in the room and Trev had wanted to hug her. He'd been none too pleased when they'd all entered the room to find her naked but he also knew her safety had to take precedence over his need to shield her from their view. Pulling her into his embrace after she was dressed, he just held her against him for several seconds before turning her into Jameson's arms.

Trev felt a deep sense of satisfaction as he watched his brother kiss the top of Kit's head and then just hold her tightly against his chest and breathe her in. Their enhanced sense of smell meant there wasn't a single nuance that would go unnoticed. The scent coming from Kit wasn't arousal, it was pure contentment and that was certainly a step in the right direction.

Jameson's words echoed his own, "I can't tell you how good you feel in my arms, kitten. I was so worried about you. I can't even imagine my life without you in it now." *'She's fucking perfect. I just want to hold her and protect her. But we need to get downstairs and find out what we're dealing with.'*

CHAPTER EIGHTEEN

K IT LET THE Wolf brothers lead her to the top of the beautiful winding wooden staircase, which led downstairs to their spacious main floor office. When they reached the top of the stairs, she looked down and sighed because she knew her legs just wouldn't carry her any further. Both Jameson and Trev had been touching her so they had both realized immediately when she'd stopped. She just stood for long seconds and stared down the stairs before she realized Jameson was speaking to her.

"Kitten? Are you alright?" When she raised her gaze to meet his, she saw his expression was filled with the same concern she'd heard in his voice.

She hated feeling weak and if she'd had the energy, she would have been angry that she felt as if she'd been totally drained. She felt the tears flood her eyes and all she manage to say was "I'm sorry, I just can't do it. My legs won't cooperate. I want to go down and give everyone the information they need, but I'm just sapped."

She felt Trev's arms come around her from behind and his warm breath against her ear, "Baby, we'll always be right beside you." She felt herself melting back into his embrace and wanted nothing more than to curl up be-tween them and sleep for a few hours. But she also knew she wouldn't really rest until she'd told everyone her story and listened to what her mother and grandmother had to say. But truthfully, it wasn't a lack of desire to help, it was just she couldn't get her feet to move down the stairs and if they had decided to try, Kit was fairly certain her legs wouldn't be on board anyway. Her entire body felt as if the energy had been siphoned out of it.

She hadn't even realized she'd closed her eyes until she felt Jameson smooth her hair behind her ear. His touch was so gentle she leaned into his calloused palm. When she opened her eyes, she felt a sudden surge of electricity race through her entire body. It was as if their souls had suddenly been welded together by the arc. In that moment the decision was made. She wanted to be their mate and the sooner the better. Just as she opened her mouth to speak the words, Jameson slammed his mouth over hers. And that is when she heard him for the first time as his voice sounded clearly in her mind. *'Mine! You belong to us, kitten, from now until the end of time.'*

When he finally came up for air, he leaned down and scooped her into his arms before starting down the stairs. "Kitten, the next time you need to be cared for—in any way—Trev and I will expect you to tell us. Your failure to ask for our help will not be allowed...ever. Now, let's get this meeting done, because as I'm sure you just heard, brother, we have a mate to claim tonight."

"Baby, the next time you don't ask for help when you need it, you're going to get a paddling that will definitely help you remember it in the future." Kit had no idea why Trev's words sent a flood of moisture to her suddenly swollen sex, but they certainly did.

"Fuck, Trev. I think our mate likes that idea because her scent just went over me like a tsunami. This may be the shortest meeting in history." Jameson's words soothed her, because it was obvious he wasn't surprised or upset that Trev's words had elicited such a strong response. For the first time she didn't feel like she was on the outside looking in when it came to men, as it had been the case so often in her very limited dating experience.

When she looked up at Trev, she noticed he was grinning at her like a loon. "You're puzzled about your body's response to my promise to spank your bare ass until it blushes a beautiful hot pink aren't you, baby?" When she nodded, he continued, "Once we start training you, we'll require you to always use words to answer, babe. But right now, I just want you to know that my brother and I consider your sweet body's response to be absolutely perfect."

They'd reached the door of their office and Jameson set her gently on her feet. She sent him a grateful smile for not carrying her into the meeting. No matter how exhausted she felt, she knew she needed to walk into the room on her own. It was important to her the members of their pack respect her because she instinctively knew everything she did or said from this point on would be a direct reflection on both Jameson and Trev. And there was a part of her that suddenly cared very much about pleasing them.

Entering their office she was surprised to see how many people were already seated in the spacious room. Jameson moved to his large, leather office chair behind the massive carved oak table he used for a desk. He pulled a chair close to his own before seating her in it then taking his own seat. Trev flanked her on the other side, keeping his hand on her shoulder. "Thanks for coming on such short notice everyone. I want you to all know how much I appreciate it. Trev and I have already provided Tristan a detailed report and I know he's combined that with his own and sent that to all of you before we came in. So, let's get Kit's eye witness account and then we'll work from there."

When he turned to her, she saw nothing but warmth in his dark eyes. "Kit, please start at the beginning and tell us exactly what happened with as much detail as you can, please." She felt him slide his large hand around her smaller one and she hadn't even realized how tightly she'd been clenching her hands together until that moment. The warmth of his fingers seemed to melt the cold in her fingers just as it was melting her fear of their mating. She couldn't ever remember feeling as cherished as she did right in this moment.

Feeling Trev move his arm so he was drawing soothing circles slowly over her lower back helped Kit focus and she appreciated their support more than she knew how to tell them. She drew in a deep breath and then told everyone everything she could remember. While she'd been speaking, her mother had been pretending to study a small sculpture on the fireplace mantel, but when Kit mentioned the man had been trying to speak into her mind, she saw her mother's attention jerk to her.

"What? Kathleen, you should have started at this point in the story. Tell me exactly how his voice sounded to you and precisely what his words were." Kit was instantly annoyed with her mother. How dare she reprimand her in front of her mates and their pack.

Kit felt her whole body stiffen and then heard Jameson's voice in her mind, *'Kitten, it's okay. Everyone in his room appreciates having each piece of the information and you have done exactly as I asked you to do.'* When she jerked her eyes to his she felt like she was suddenly falling ass over teakettle into their dark depths. *'Shifters can speak telepathically when their bonds are strong, so everyone in the room that*

I'm allowing in is able to hear my words to you. And to answer the questions I see in your eyes, no your mother is blocked, but your grandmother is not. I have not blocked your father either. And yes, Trev can hear and speak to you already as well.'

Kit looked up and smiled at her grandmother and father who both subtly nodded their heads at her. She was suddenly almost overwhelmed with feelings of belonging that she'd never before experienced, but had always longed for. That same look of acceptance was reflected in the faces of the others in the room, most of whom she hadn't even actually met yet. She tried to push her thanks through her mind and could only hope they had all been able to hear how grateful she was for their support.

Looking up, she met her mother's gaze head on. "I have done exactly as Jameson asked me to do, Mother. Now, as I was saying, the man seemed to be trying to recruit me. I can't remember his exact words, because it was more like he was trying to get inside my head and change my way of thinking. And for some reason I had the feeling he felt the plea would be more persuasive before I mated."

Kit let her eyes track ever so briefly to her grandmother and noticed her almost imperceptible nod. Kit returned her attention to her mother and saw her wrinkled brow. "Kathleen, tell me exactly how you reacted and how on earth you managed to shatter bullet-proof glass with your little fit of angry magic." The sarcasm dripped from her mother's words, and they also seemed laced with jealousy. It was certainly a side of her mother Kit had never seen before.

"I don't really know exactly how it happened. I knew he was going to hurt my mates. I saw his hand raised and the wand in it pointed at the door I could hear being unlocked. I raised my hand to block his action and there was a huge flash of light then I heard glass shattering. The next instant the man evaporated. It was if he just blew apart into a mist that slowly drifted away." She remembered wondering how a body could just vaporize into something that looked like a dense fog but she'd let it go, because when she considered that he'd been floating in mid-air, anything after that seemed inconsequential.

Kit watched as her mother paced back and forth in front of the fireplace for what seemed like several minutes. No one made a move to stop her and no one spoke to her either. It was if everyone sensed her need to process the information Kit had given her. Just when Kit was getting ready to speak again, her mother spun and looked at her own mother. "What do you think? Is it possible he got through the lock we put on the portal gate? Goddess, it was the strongest one we've ever done. I didn't think he'd be able to breach it for another century at least."

Kit watched in wonder as the timid, elderly woman she'd always believed her grandmother to be shifted right in front of her into a stunningly beautiful woman. Everyone in the room gasped at the transformation and Kit saw the corners of her father's lips twitch at the annoyed look on his wife's face.

"Very dramatic, Mother, now if you wouldn't mind answering the question it would be most helpful." Kit heard the frustration in her mother's voice and if she wasn't mistaken, that had been exactly what her grandmother had been going for. In her entire life, Kit had never seen her grandmother in her "witch's finery" as her grandfather had always referred to it.

Just thinking about the grandfather who had filled her life with such joy sent a sharp pain of loneliness through her heart that nearly stole her breath. When Trev moved his hand to her waist and pulled her close, she felt herself being brought back to the moment and she appreciated the fact he'd known she needed his connection. "Baby, we're with you every step of the way and I'm sure that sweet grandfather of yours is looking down on you and beaming with pride. Hell, he had a hot wife *and* granddaughter." When Kit looked over at him he waggled his eyebrows at her making her giggle, and Goddess she loved him for it. *Loved? Oh wicked wands, where had that thought come from?* His and Jameson's laughter told her that she had evidently been thinking at full volume.

Ruby Stone's voice moved through the room like a choir of angels, and Kit couldn't remember ever hearing her grandmother sounding so resolute in her incantations. The protection spell she cast was one Kit had heard many times but she'd never seen her grandmother's true power as a witch before this moment. As the spell ended, eddies of glowing glitter seemed to swirl through the room before surrounding Kit and her mates. Once the sparkles had finally subsided, Kit looked at her grandmother and raised her brow. When the witch merely shrugged her shoulders, Kit almost burst out laughing. Here was the woman she always thought stood in her own daughter's shadow but now, Kit knew her grandmother was, in fact, clearly the stronger of the two witches. And with casual nonchalance she was acting as if what she'd just done was nothing more than baking a batch of cookies for the neighborhood kids.

Immediately Kit felt a lightness all around her and an infusion of energy that could only described as electric. She didn't feel drained as she had just a few minutes earlier so she knew the spell had probably been infused with some kind of energy boost as well. When she looked at her grandmother, Kit saw the twinkle in her eye, and then her wink had confirmed Kit's suspicions.

As if on cue, Ruby turned to her daughter, "I'm not entirely surprised he managed to find another way out. And Kit's magic is much stronger than any of us imagined, so she has set him back several years by *scrambling his molecular makeup* so to speak." Her words were met with chuckles from around the room. "What we don't want to do is let our guard down, because I can promise you…this is not over. It may take them a few months to re-group because Damian isn't really dead."

Kit saw the confused looks on the faces of the others in the room and figured they weren't much different from her own. She was grateful her grandmother continued her explanation without pause, "Oh he's been set back for sure. And personally I'm thrilled that he so grossly underestimated Kit's abilities…serves the asshat right." Her devious grin warmed Kit's heart and she found herself moving to her grandmother and pulling her into a hug.

Kit whispered against her grandmother's ear, "Thank you…for believing in me and for showing me this side of you. Grandfather always told me this woman was just beneath the surface and that I'd see her when the time was right. I want you to know how much I love you."

When Ruby pulled back, she moved Kit's hair over her shoulders just as she always had when Kit had been a little girl and the gesture brought back a flood of sweet memories of all the time she'd spent with her grandparents. "Kit, your magical abilities are so far advanced of your mother's and mine that I have every confidence you'll be fine as long as you always stay on the this side of the *light* and avoid dark magic at all costs. I want to caution you that resisting it isn't as easy it sounds. Don't ever scoff at the dark side's ability to trick you or to temp you with promises that appeal to desires even you didn't know you harbored."

Her grandmother pulled her close and Kit saw her raise her hand and with a flick of her wrist they were both encased in a swirling cloud of sparkling white. It was the most amazing thing Kit had ever seen. On the inside everything was clear and eerily quiet, but the glittering white cloud encircling them was buzzing softly. Ruby laughed and said, "The quiet spell I used on your mother isn't going to last much longer, so we need to wrap this up. I wanted to tell you that your men's hearts are golden. They are your true mates and the sooner you are formally mated the safer you will be. Even though this mating was foretold, they did not know that, and it plays no part in their desire for you." The feel of her grandmother's fingers along the side of her face was so comforting, Kit wanted to close her eyes and just lose herself in the sensation. "Trust your instincts, Kit. And trust your mates. Always remember I'll be here to teach and guide for as long as you need me, but then I'm planning to join your grandfather on the other side of the veil. He's waiting for me." Suddenly the sweet elderly woman that Kit knew as her grandmother was back and she winked at Kit, "We have plans you know, it's not just you young people who enjoy sex."

While Kit was still lost in everything she'd been told, the swirling mist dropped like a heavy fog and there was nothing left but a few sparkles of glitter around them on the rug. When she looked up both Jameson and Trev were coming toward her with intense looks on their faces. She wasn't sure if they were angry they'd been shut out or worried about what had taken place, but their desire to assure themselves she was all right was evident.

Jameson reached her first and pulled her tightly against

his chest. "Are you okay, kitten? That was an amazing cocoon your sweet granny created. And later I want you to tell us all about it. But right now, my brother and I have other plans for you. We'll wrap this up quickly and then we're going upstairs." Kit shivered as Jameson's last words were actually more growled than spoken.

Trev echoed his brother's concern, but his smile told her that he was equally impressed. "Your grandmother is one hot chick when she shifts, baby." Despite his teasing tone, Kit could hear the concern in his voice and she turned into his arms, wrapped her arms around his waist, and just drew upon his strength for long seconds. When she finally pulled back and looked up at him, he asked, "We need to make you ours, baby. Are you ready for that?"

As she nodded her head she remembered their earlier admonishment that she needed to answer using words so she spoke her assent quietly but clearly, "Yes, I'm ready. I belonged to both of you from the first moment I met you. And even though I was trying to avoid finding my mates, I'm awfully glad fate had other ideas." Right now there wasn't anything she wanted more than to have Jameson and Trev claim her. She no longer feared belonging to them.

Just as they stepped out into the hallway, Libby ran up to her and hugged her tight. "Holy shit on the Schmidt house, Kit. Do you know these people are shifters? It is totally fucking cool. And you're sleeping with the two leaders? You go girl." Libby gave her a fist bump and winked at her. Kit knew her tiny tornado friend was one of the smartest people she had ever known, and certainly the most loyal friend she'd ever had so Kit wasn't worried Libby would spill the beans back at the university. She did however worry about the *interrogation* each and every member of the Wolf's pack was about to be subjected to.

"Do you know how long it took me to figure this out? Good God that hottie your Jameson glued to me...seriously, they should call him Elmer. Well, he wouldn't let me out of his sight long enough for me to work it through until I finally *persuaded* him to let me at least go to the john alone. Damn, that window out of the shower in my room is fucking high I tell you, took every towel in there to boost me high enough to shimmy through. Luckily there is a nice walkway that runs around this massive place they call a house...on all the floors and I learned a lot of interesting things strolling by various windows before Elmer found me. Oh, Peeping Tom has nothing on me sister...not a thing...nada." Good God, Libby was in rare form tonight. Kit was starting to giggle at her friend's exuberance. She wondered what she was going to think when she had all the facts. And Kit didn't doubt for a single moment that Libby Wells wasn't going to rest until she knew each and every minute detail.

CHAPTER NINETEEN

WATCHING KIT SMILE at her pint-sized friend as the little blonde chattered a mile-a-minute, Jameson's heart warmed. Not only was their mate smart and gorgeous, she was kind and that made her a thousand times more attractive in his book any day. He was going to enjoy teasing Charlie about losing Dr. Libby Wells, but then again, he wasn't sure their very best security could have contained the determined young woman. Jameson used his telepathic link to let Charlie know it was time to distract his exuberant charge so they could get Kit upstairs. The young man blushed, but quickly nodded in understanding.

When he and Trev finally closed the door of their suite, Jameson was almost ready to come out of his skin his need to claim her was so great. "Kit, it's important that you understand exactly what's about to happen—neither Trev nor I want there to be any secrets between us and that starts right now." He could hear every beat of her heart and knew she was close to losing the last of her control. "And as much as we both want to strip you and claim you before we even walk across the room, we want what is best for you even more."

Trev stepped up to stand beside him and nodded. "That's right, baby, claiming is really a two-step process. Well, the actual act is one step, but there is a formal part that will occur at midnight on the next full moon." Jameson watched as Kit's eyes widened and he knew they needed to handle this next part carefully.

Jameson took her small hand in his, led her over to the sofa, and settled her on his lap facing Trev who sat next to them. "There is a more political aspect of mating when the Alpha of a pack is involved, love." He took a deep breath and just forged ahead, "We'll have to claim you again when we are all in our wolf. This takes place in the meadow and anyone in our pack who wants to attend is welcome to do so." He saw her eyes go wide with understanding just before she began to tremble. Wrapping his arms around her, he pulled her against his chest. "Kitten, I'm not going to mislead you, I think there will be quite a number of people in attendance when we do this. They won't be there as voyeurs per se, but the mating of a pack's Alpha is considered an historic event because it only happens once every generation, so it will be seen as a joyful event to celebrate."

"You mean members of your pack will come out to the meadow and watch you and Trev...um...take me? Oh my God, I can't even imagine doing that." Jameson's heart sank at her words. And the look of defeat and loss in her eyes was gut wrenching, but it was the fact she wasn't trusting them to protect and care for her that hurt him the most.

"Kit, do you remember how protective Trev and I were about you being seen by members of our security team in this very room, not once, but on two different occasions?" When she nodded he continued, "And, did you hear me say you would be in your wolf during the meadow ceremony? Because, my love, there is no way we'd ever let anyone see us making love to you while you are in your human form." He couldn't help the growl that vibrated through his chest because even thinking about his pack seeing his mate naked was enough to make his vision go red with rage. He heard a similar sound from his twin and knew Kit had noticed when she glanced between them.

Jameson watched as Kit took several steadying breaths and then seemed to shake off her thoughts. "I'm sorry I panicked. It is all just so new to me and even though my parents are shifters, I've never been around a pack, so your traditions are a complete mystery to me." She had been looking directly at first one, then the other as she'd spoken, but when she continued, her gaze dropped to her lap. "I'm glad you told me. I know you probably didn't have to do that, but I want you to know that I appreciate the fact you didn't go all Alpha on me and just 'fuck me into submission' like my mother encouraged you to do."

Jameson was shocked that she'd heard her mother's crude remark and his heart twisted when he saw a teardrop fall onto her hands, which were clasped tightly in her lap. Using his finger to raise her gaze to meet his, Jameson wished with everything in him that his sweet mate hadn't been exposed to the hurtful comment. "Kit, your mother shouldn't have said that, and she particularly shouldn't have said it when you were obviously close enough to hear her. For what it's worth, I think she truly does have your best interest at heart, even if her method of showing it is not terribly impressive. I also want you to rest assured, since your parents aren't members of our pack, they won't be allowed in the meadow for the claiming ceremony."

Seeing her relief made him glad he'd made a point to mention the fact neither of her parents would be allowed to witness the ceremony that would take place in just a few hours, despite the fact they would likely still be at the estate. *'Let's get her into bed and claim her before something else happens, brother.*' Trev's voice pushed through Jameson's thoughts and for once, he was glad for the intrusion. He nodded and picked Kit up and walked to the bed.

Setting their woman on her feet, he stepped back so he stood alongside Trev. "Strip, Kit. We're going to make you ours in the same way it's been done among shifters for centuries." Watching her shaking hands pull her shirt up over her head, he had to make a conscious effort to take a breath as her breasts were uncovered exposing her already peaked nipples to their view. *Fuck me, she is perfect. And I can't wait to sink into her sweet ass.*

It was pack tradition that the Alpha take his mate's ass and bite her right shoulder. Jameson knew Trev would be deep in her wet cunt and would be sinking his teeth deep in her left shoulder a split second after Jameson's own fangs pierced her skin. And as much as he hated the fact their bites were going to hurt her, he also knew she would only feel the pain for a few seconds before their DNA merged with her own and the pain was replaced by blinding pleasure.

Jameson stood with his legs apart and his arms crossed over his chest as his brother stripped and pulled Kit into his arms. Watching his brother kiss their mate was almost as good as kissing her himself because he felt the emotions that swirled through Trev's mind. Smelling her pussy flood with her sweet cream, Jameson growled when he realized that she had just come into heat. Closing his eyes to savor the slight change in her scent, Jameson felt Trev's pleasure as he came to the same realization.

EVERY CELL IN Trev's body went on alert the instant the

slight change in her scent washed through his nose. Knowing their mate was now in heat would amp up their desire for her exponentially and letting her out of bed had already been a constant challenge. Kneeling in front of Kit, Trev leaned forward and lapped at her bare pussy lips. He noticed there was already a slight difference in her honey. It was a stronger scent and the flavor was more "earthy" in its taste. He nudged her legs further apart and leaned her back so her bare ass cheeks were right at the edge of their bed. Sliding his tongue over and through her wet folds he could feel her body ramping itself up as she closed in on her release. But each time he knew she was nearly there he backed off just enough to keep her on edge, because he wasn't ready to send her over the edge yet.

"Don't you dare come until one of your mates tells you to, baby. We want to give you an experience that will send you higher than you even knew was possible. But in order to do that, we need for you to hold it off as long as possible." He felt her legs tremble, but she hadn't actually responded. Trev watched Jameson step up beside Kit and lower his face to her breasts and pull one and then the other nipple into his mouth. Trev could see his brother was biting down just hard enough to send a zing of pain racing through her system. Seeing her reaction to the pain and her moans of desire as the pain morphed into pleasure was enough to make Trev pause before he lost control of his own release. Shooting semen all over the satin-smooth skin of her leg wasn't at all what he had planned.

"Baby, you are going to drive me completely out of my mind if I don't get inside you." Trev quickly reversed their positions and leaned back against the very edge of the bed. Pulling Kit into his arms, he didn't waste any time picking her up and sliding her down onto his throbbing cock, and in one swift thrust, he felt his cock head press against her cervix. Resting his forehead against hers, Trev locked his eyes on Kit's and let the growl he'd been fighting rumble up through his chest. When she tilted her head back, exposing the long line of her slender throat, the significance of the move wasn't lost on him. *'She's ready, brother. Let's make her ours forever.'*

Chapter Twenty

J AMESON HADN'T THOUGHT he could want Kit any more until he'd seen her lean her head back and bare her throat when she'd heard Trev's growl. He knew the move had likely been pure instinct, and that made it even more significant in Jameson's view. The overt act of surrendering to her mates made his heart stutter for a moment as he felt the weight of the emotion move through him. Seeing her make herself completely vulnerable to Trev almost brought Jameson to his knees.

Hearing Trev's words in his mind brought him back to the moment and he stepped up behind Kit and smoothed his hands over her soft shoulders. Massaging the tension from her shoulders and upper back for a few minutes gave them both a chance to prepare for what was to come. "Kitten, your trust humbles me. Knowing you are giving yourself to us and joining your life with ours is the best gift I've ever received."

Trev leaned back on the bed and spread his legs wide making a space for Jameson to step into and also opening Kit's ass to his view. Looking down at the tight rosette of her rear hole, Jameson was already fighting his wolf's most basic instinct that was screaming at him to sink his cock deep and bite her staking his lifetime claim. Preparing her properly was going to be particularly important since he and Trev both needed to unleash a small part of their wolf in order to claim her. And unleashing their wolf would mean their cocks would become significantly larger so he was going to massage generous amounts of lube into her tight ass and stretch the muscles all he could. Changing was necessary because they needed their fangs elongated and sharp to pierce her soft skin cleanly and sink deeply into the muscle so their DNA would flow quickly through her system. The deeper their bite the quicker the pain would be masked by the changes mating would bring about in her body.

Jameson used the lube they'd placed on the small nightstand and rained kisses over her shoulders as he pushed through the tight ring of muscles of her ass. He continued rimming her for several minutes until she was pushing back against him before he began the slow process of fucking her sweet ass with first one finger and then adding another. When he'd gotten her to the point that he was easily moving three of his large fingers in and out of her hole, Jameson leaned over and licked her shoulder. "Your wolf calls to mine, kitten. And I can see the golden flecks in my brother's eyes and know he is fighting the same battle." Letting his wolf surface enough, he felt his cock lengthen and harden into an even wider shaft and his fangs showed themselves as he felt saliva begin to pool in his mouth. Wrapping his hand in the silky tresses, he tugged just as he pressed the tip of his cock against her rear hole.

When his cock started to breach her ass, he felt her stiffen and he growled, "Let me in, mate." He used the voice all Alphas possessed, but he rarely used its power, preferring to let pack members make their decisions—right or wrong—using their free will. But there was no turning back from their mating. When he felt her muscles push back against him, he thrust in deep, leaned forward, and sank his fangs deep into the tender skin where her neck joined her shoulder. As she was drawing in her breath to scream, he felt Trev's love for her just as his brother's actions on Kit's other side mirrored his own. Kit's scream of pain almost broke his heart, but he didn't release. Letting plenty of their saliva flow into her bloodstream so her changes would be complete was critical to a successful mating. Besides, he damned well didn't want to have to bite her again while she was in her human form.

Kit's scream was followed by a flash of brilliant white light, which seemed to sparkle as if it had been infused with dancing glitter. Jameson could literally feel the hair on his arms standing up the way it did when he was outside during a summer thunderstorms that were filled with lightning. Every candle in the room went completely out and then suddenly reignited and flared brightly before returning to normal. Kit's skin seemed to glow forever, but Jameson knew it couldn't have been longer than thirty seconds.

When he and Trev both released Kit from their mating bites, they licked the wounds tenderly. Jameson was pleased to see the puncture marks heal quickly and within a few seconds all that was left were the small scars Kit would carry for the rest of her life. Mated females wore the small marks as proudly as they would a wedding ring or BDSM collar. Jameson felt like he was floating on cloud nine as he pulled back and looked down to see his tiny mate arching her back in an effort to get them to move their cocks, which were still embedded deeply inside her sweet body. They'd just sent their saliva into her blood and knew it was coursing quickly through her system. And as the changes began, he wasn't surprised to feel the heat emanating from her smooth skin.

He smiled at Trev over her shoulder when he heard her growl just before speaking in a tone much deeper than her regular speaking voice. "Please fuck me, I need to feel you both moving inside me. My entire body feels like it is on fire and the only thing that is going to extinguish the flames is feeling your seed filling me."

Jameson froze for a split second, completely lost in his overwhelming feelings of love and pride in their mate. "Kitten, I can't even begin to tell you how pleased you have made us. Thank you for asking for what you need. We'll spend the rest of our lives protecting you, loving you, and making sure you never have a moment when you wonder if you made the right decision becoming ours." Without even speaking to his brother, they set a steady alternating push-pull rhythm so one of them had a cock deep in their mate's luscious body at all times. Feeling his own release moving on the fringes of his consciousness, Jameson nodded to Trev and they picked up the pace.

Feeling Kit's inner muscles begin to pulse, Jameson knew she was close to her release. *'Send your seed into her womb. I can't wait to see her belly swollen with our child and her breasts heavy as she prepares to nurse the babe we'll both love and raise together.'* It wouldn't matter which of them was the biological father because she was mated to them both and they would love any child of their union unconditionally. Jameson knew the instant her body launched into orgasm because her muscles locked down on his cock like a vice and pulled him right over the edge with her. Kit screamed so loud he worried she was going to be hoarse, but he was thrilled this shout was pure bliss rather than pain.

Struggling to keep from collapsing on top of his mate and brother, Jameson gasped in several deep breaths and locked his knees after an orgasm so powerful he'd actually worried he was going to pass out. He'd never felt anything that earth shattering. He'd heard his friends describe their matings, but had never realized how their bodies seemed to amplify each other's responses until they ended in a result that was nothing short of cataclysmic.

When he finally felt like he could move without crumpling into a heap, he pulled his still hard cock from Kit's ass and staggered into the bath to clean up. When he returned with a wet cloth and a dry towel, Jameson lifted Kit gently from Trev and positioned her at the edge of the bed so he could clean her before patting her dry. Before he had even finished he could hear her deep, even breathing and knew she had succumbed to the bone deep fatigue she'd been holding off since she'd vaporized the evil that had literally been floating outside their bedroom window.

When they'd settled her between them, he let the emotion of the moment wash over him. Nothing had ever felt as *right* as holding Kit in his arms. He and Trev had already commissioned her ring the first night they'd met her. They planned to propose at the celebration following her first run under the full moon later tonight. When he finally moved his eyes from Kit's angelic face, Jameson noticed Trev watching him. *'I had almost given up finding her, but even in my dreams she wasn't this amazing.'*

Jameson knew exactly what his brother was saying. Hell, they'd both almost given up finding their mate, but she was well worth the wait. *'Now we need to concentrate on keeping her safe. I know her family has said she has delayed the battle, but my gut tells me it's coming sooner rather than later.'*

He watched Trev lean forward and press his nose against Kit's flat abdomen and inhale. Trev's smile said it all, the changes in Kit's body had already started. Their child was resting safely beneath her heart and Jameson knew they were equally thrilled with the fact. *'I want to marry her yesterday.'* Jameson couldn't help but chuckle at his brother's impatience.

"How is a girl to get any sleep with you two yammering away?" Kit's words were laced with laughter, and he and Trev both looked up to see her looking thoughtfully between them. "So, I'm assuming by that little sniff you did over my tummy you are either enamored by my use of your shower gel or you've already managed to knock me up."

He and Trev both frowned at Kit and Jameson growled at her crude description of what he considered beautiful. "You need to rephrase that mate—*quickly*—before the fathers of the little bundle of joy take exception to your crass remark." He was pleased to see her cheeks blush in embarrassment as she looked them both in the eyes and apologized. With that out of the way, Jameson looked deeply into Kit's eyes and asked, "Do you feel any different now, kitten?"

Kit considered the question but really didn't notice any difference. "No, I don't and I wonder why you can tell and I can't."

"Your senses of smell and vision will gradually become sharper over the next few weeks. The changes from mating don't all happen overnight. And kitten, I don't really know exactly how your magical abilities will affect your changes, but I must admit I'm definitely curious. Now, what do you say to a run under the stars? I'm dying to see you in your wolf." Jameson couldn't wait to mate her again under the stars while they were both in their wolf form. Even thinking about how she was going to feel under him as he slid deep into her throbbing cunt was enough to make his dick rock hard. Using his teeth at her nape to hold her down as he pumped in and out of her while the moon acted as their spotlight.

They gave her a t-shirt and a loose pair of shorts to wear on the way downstairs but warned her that once she was on the back deck, she would be expected to strip just like the others. "There is no modesty there, kitten. We're all in the same boat, so it's not a big deal to us. We know you will be uncomfortable at first, but you'll get used to it soon enough." At her puzzled expression, he grinned. "I know it seems inconsistent to you and I suppose in some ways you are right. But being naked just before you change along with the others is much different from you being naked in our bedroom." He hadn't really considered how hypocritical it was before this moment. And in the end it didn't matter, because it just was what it was.

Jameson could tell Kit wasn't convinced she was going to ever be as blasé about being nude in front of the other members of their pack, but she evidently wasn't going to argue the point either. There were only a few pack members on the deck when they arrived and Jameson was pleased to see most of them were women. Just before they stepped through the door, Trev stopped her and spoke into her mind. *'Baby, remember that Jameson is your Alpha. Follow his lead and obey his instructions because you are going to be watched closely.'*

Chapter Twenty-One

TREV'S WORDS REGISTERED in her mind at the same time Kit saw a young woman with long black hair standing along the rail watching her through narrowed eyes. *Oh yeah, being watched indeed. Can anyone say awkward moment? Geez, Kit, you had to know men this gorgeous were going to have ex-girlfriends. Suck it up buttercup and make your mates proud of you.* She'd hoped they wouldn't hear the pep talk she'd given herself, but judging by the grins on their faces that didn't appear to be the case.

As they walked among the others, Kit felt their scrutiny and wished she could just turn around and march back up the stairs. But she stiffened her spine and reminded herself that she could be a victor or a victim, the choice was hers and it was a slam-dunk decision. *'Good girl, run to the roar.'* Kit smiled at Trev in thanks as his words moved into her mind.

Jameson stepped in front of her, turned his back to the other pack members, and crossed his arms over chest after shucking his shirt. "Strip, kitten. I want to see you naked before we start talking you through your first change." Kit felt as if someone had dropped a piano on her chest and for a few seconds she stood blinking at him in surprise before she quickly pulled the shirt over her head and pushed the shorts to the floor. Seeing his nostrils flare and his eyes turn molten with desire sent a flood of moisture to her sex. She hoped her gratitude that he'd blocked her from the view of the others showed in her eyes as she waited patiently for his next instruction.

Trev's voice was almost a benediction behind her. "Fuck, baby, you are so damned hot. Let's get this done so we can get out to the meadow and play."

Jameson stripped out of his shorts and his erection told Kit how much he wanted her and that along with the feel of the scorching head of Trev's cock pressing into her ass as he leaned against her buoyed her confidence. Jameson's fingers trailed a scorching path down her cheek and she refocused her attention on him. "Good girl, kitten. Now, I need you to pay very close attention to what I tell you. The first few times you change it may be uncomfortable and we can minimize that if you'll do exactly what I tell you."

Kit found herself unable to look away from his eyes and the sound of his voice had her attention riveted. "Okay, my love, changing is all about mind over matter. I want you to close your eyes and listen to my voice. Perfect. God, you do me in." Kit heard him take several deep breaths and she felt him step closer. The heat from his body soaked into her chest and Trev's warmth spread over her back. "Now in your mind see how your beautiful red hair becomes a slick coat of fur that shines even the dimmest of light. Feel the wind as it rushes over your face as you run just for the joy of running. The breeze brings with it all the wonders of the woods that surround us and you know by instinct where your mates are at all times. You feel them running alongside you and relish in the feeling that you share a secret that our kind has cherished and protected since the dawn of time."

Kit was hypnotized by Jameson's words and felt her body start to change almost immediately. He'd kept speaking over the popping of her joints and her soft gasps of pain as she felt the muscles stretch and lengthen. For a second she felt herself slipping out of the web Jameson had spun around her with his words, but Trev's teeth scraped over her shoulder and brought her attention back to the moment. When she felt herself drop to all fours, she was hit by a wave of euphoria that she couldn't hold back.

She went over the railing in a smooth leap and hit the ground running. Jameson had been right about every single thing he'd said and for a moment she wondered if maybe he had seen the future. She could feel them running alongside her as well as see them. Her vision was so sharp and she was thrilled to be able to see so clearly in the dark. For several minutes she just ran as hard as she could because the feel of the air on her face and ruffling through her fur was electrifying.

She felt Jameson's presence in her mind, heeded his directions, and veered to the left. She realized she was in the middle of a moonlit meadow so she slowed and eventually stopped. The feeling of her two mates rubbing themselves against her in loving passes along her sides had her lowering her front shoulders and arching her back. Kit was overcome with awareness of her own instincts taking over. She was thrilled to realize she could easily tell her mates apart even though they were as identical in their wolf as they were as humans. When Jameson pressed his nose against her sex and sniffed before howling she felt a whole new flood of moisture and wanted nothing more than for them to fill her with their cocks.

Chapter Twenty-Two

TALKING KIT THROUGH her first change had been much easier than Jameson had thought it might be. Her independence and intelligence could have easily been barriers to her letting her mind take a backseat to the instinct he'd known was deep inside her. But she'd let him lead her and he'd been so proud of her when she'd gone over the tall railing surrounding the deck without even taking a step. He and Trev had been right behind her and seeing her hit the hard earth with such grace had been truly spectacular.

He and Trev had laughed with each other as they'd run. And even though they hadn't specifically excluded Kit from the conversation, he'd known she was so busy absorbing everything happening to and around her that she had tuned them out. *'She is having the time of her life.'* Trev's voice was filled with amusement.

'That she is, but it's time to get her attention and steer her into the meadow. I don't want her too tired to enjoy what's to come. And she still has to run all the way home.' Jameson knew Kit thought she'd run in a straight line, but they had actually gently guided her in a wide arc. If they had gone that same distance without turning they would have traveled almost fifteen miles. When Kit stopped in the meadow and lowered her head and front shoulders in submission, Jameson and Trev both howled in triumph.

Jameson positioned himself behind Kit and licked her pussy several times before rolling his tongue and fucking her with it so she was soaking wet and stretched to accommodate his cock. It was going to be like taking her virginity again because her wolf had never been fucked. The difference was that it wasn't the way of the wolf to be gentle. This mating would be fast and hard. To an outsider it would even look violent, but the ways of animals was more about survival of the fittest. The Alphas needed to show their dominance in order to maintain their credibility as the leaders of their pack—it had always been this since the dawn of time.

'Kitten, I know your body is ready for mine and I'm claiming what is mine to take. You'll get soft and slow later, right now, I'm taking what is mine.' Before she would even respond he bit her nape and slammed in as far as he could go. *'Your body belongs to me, Kit. Surrender your pleasure to me. Take what I give you.'* As soon as he bit down hard enough to pierce her skin, she came around him in almost painful contractions of her cunt. Seeing the sparks of electrical power that sparkled around them let Jameson know her magical powers would be available to her when she was in her wolf also and he found that oddly comforting. He was able to hold out for several more strokes before he followed her into bliss. When he pulled out, he rubbed his nose in their combined fluids and then moved in front of her to smear it over her nose so their scents would remain imprinted on her for the rest of her life.

TREV STEPPED UP behind Kit and positioned his cock at the entrance of her ass. When he felt her tense in front of his tip, he let the growl rumble through his chest. *'Let me in, mate. Your ass is mine to claim. Push back against me and surrender what is mine.'* Trev was glad Kit didn't know they were mating with witnesses because he knew how unsettled she'd been by the idea earlier. They'd let her believe it was scheduled for a couple of nights from now, but the process was nearly complete.

If they had waited her sense of smell would have been developed enough to note the others standing just at the edge of the trees. Trev had been less than happy to see several of the female members of their pack that he and Jameson had shared turn out to watch them mate with Kit. They were required to keep their communication with her open during this first mating and that meant everyone was watching *and listening* with avid interest. Their dominance over their mate would be discussed for years. He understood that it was imperative to them being respected as pack leaders, but he hated having anything about fucking his mate dictated by law rather than her needs. They'd been much more aggressive and course than they preferred with Kit, but her response to their gruff words and aggressive actions had surprised and pleased both he and Jameson.

Trev pushed deep into her ass, clamped his teeth at her nape, and bit down hard so his canines pierced her skin. He tasted her blood and the taste of her blood went over his taste buds and sent his arousal off the chart. Trev pulled out until the head of his cock was ready to pop out of the tight ring around Kit's ass before he pushed back in deep. He immediately heard her in his mind, her soft moans were total surrender and his mind shouted into hers. *'Come with me, baby. Surrender your pleasure to your mate. Give it to me. Now.'*

Kit's back arched to the point that her ass looked like it was being presented in offering for his pleasure and he felt her shatter under him. Her total submission triggered a volcanic eruption that began in his balls and exploded out of the end of his cock in hot jets of his semen. He pulled out and shot some of the seed over her ass and then smeared it with his nose before rubbing it against her snout just as Jameson had done. Her mind would carry that memory for the rest of her life. And even if one of them was killed, she would always be able to pull that scent memory back and relive this moment.

Trev felt Kit go lax beneath him and he panted for long moments before he was able to stand without his legs swaying beneath him. *'You own me, baby. You are now our mate in every way. Centuries of tradition have bound your soul to ours so tightly that neither time nor trial will ever be able to separate us.'* Jameson howled to their left and Trev looked up to see they'd been circled by the witnesses. He saw the recognition in her eyes and pushed against her in a move he hoped conveyed the affection of a hug.

The pack broke the circle and took off running in various directions leaving the three of them to enjoy a moment alone. *'That was our witnessed mating?'* Kit's voice was clear in their minds and Trev could hear the unspoken questions as well.

'Yes, kitten. We thought you'd be less nervous this way. I'm sorry if you feel we tricked you. We were trying to help.' Jameson obviously hadn't missed her tension either. *'Now, are you ready to return to our home? I know I speak for my brother as well when I say that I want to take you home so we can care for you and our child. And even though we know that you won the first battle, I'm sure we all agree the war is still to come.'*

'Sadly, I'm afraid you are right. But I'm not going to waste

the joy I'm feeling in this moment by worrying about it.' Trev was so caught up in her words that he almost missed the slight twitch in her muscles that signaled her intent. But he couldn't be angry because her laughter echoed through his mind and it was filled with pure child-like joy as she raced for their home and he couldn't help but laugh.

'My love for her feels like fire raging through every cell in my body. I know our friends tried to explain it, but this is so much more than I ever imagined it to be.' Jameson's words were a perfect description of how he felt. And as they watched her take the lead as they ran toward their home and future, Trev tried to put aside his worries about the battles he knew she would face and just enjoy the feeling of exhilaration he always felt as the wind rushed over his fur. The moon and stars seemed to be working in tandem to light their way and he could only hope those celestial spirits continued to guide them through the years to come.

EPILOGUE

Eight Months Later

K IT LOOKED OVER her well-rounded belly as the twins nestled safely inside seemed to battle for position. Letting her gaze settle on the top of the pool's sparkling water, she watched as the sunshine sparkled over the rippling surface. "It looks like diamonds. Lord love a leper but I do love diamonds." When she looked over the top of her sunglasses at her friends, they were all staring at her as if she'd just grown another head. "What?"

It wasn't a surprise that Libby was the first to speak, "Are you fucking kidding me? This is newsworthy information? Fuck me, you are annoying sometimes." Libby's giggle betrayed the fact her words were spoken in jest.

"Agreed. Her husbands spoil her shamelessly and I'd be plotting her demise if she wasn't knocked up. I can't kill babies, that just wouldn't be right...killing a diamond slut is something else entirely." Julie Wolf-Edwards was a cousin to Jameson and Trev and one of the most outspoken women Kit had ever met. She was a Harvard trained lawyer who handled all the pack's legal work and Kit had never seen the woman miss a single detail in anything she'd tackled. She was also a classic beauty with chestnut colored hair that she kept cut in a stylish bob and glorious hazel eyes that were always filled with mischief.

Julie was married to Lance Edwards who was an

enormously popular television actor and one of the few non-shifters living in the mansion even though he occasionally stayed at their loft in So-Ho on nights when he'd been working late. But more than once, Kit had seen Lance coming in during the wee hours of the morning. She'd asked him once why he'd driven so far at that time of night and he'd smiled conspiratorially. "Are you kidding? My wife is fucking *hot* and brilliant and my best friend. Why wouldn't I want to be in her bed?" Kit had fallen a little bit in love with him herself at that moment. She'd always liked him as an actor, he reminded her of Robert Redford in "Butch Cassidy and the Sundance Kid. And finding out what a genuinely nice man he was had only made her like him more.

"Well?" Kit looked at Angie Michaels expectantly. "Aren't you going to add anything to the peanut gallery's litany of sarcasm?"

Angie tilted her head back and flipped her blonde ponytail over her shoulder. "Nope, they've got this."

They all giggled and settled back to enjoy a few minutes where the only sounds were those made by the small waterfall at the other end of the pool and the breeze whispering through the nearby trees. Suddenly Kit felt like someone had thrown a glass of ice water over her and she felt herself starting to panic. There didn't seem to be any logical explanation for the sudden change, but then she heard it again and realized her sub-conscious had registered the words whispering on the wind even when she hadn't noticed them the first time.

Soon... We'll meet again, soon. I'm coming for you. Joining me will make you a Princess of the Darkness and the pleasures of the world will be yours for the taking. Your children will belong to me. Our combined power will be unstoppable. Don't fight this, Kathleen. It is your destiny. Are you willing to sacrifice your friends to deny me what is mine to take?

Kit fought his hold on her mind and suddenly snapped back to the moment. She was covered in a fine sheen of moisture from the cold sweat she'd experienced and she was shaking so hard she was worried she might fall off the lounge chair she'd been relaxing on just moments ago. All three of her friends had gathered around her and she could see the concerned looks on their faces but she couldn't seem to pull herself up from the fear that was threatening to overtake her.

Kit had learned many years ago that it was a curse to even entertain the thought that things couldn't get any worse, because the Universe seemed all too willing to prove otherwise. But just as she was wondering how things had gone wrong so quickly her phone played "Witchy Woman" by The Eagles, the ringtone for her mother, and Kit groaned. She was still debating whether or not to answer the call when Jameson and Trevlon both ran around the corner. Kit tried not to let the stark terror she felt at Damian's threats to their children and friends take root, but she also knew the seeds of fear had already been planted the night she'd seen him floating outside their bedroom window. She also knew she should be grateful for the reprieve she'd experienced during the past eight months, but the truth was she had hoped it would last a lot longer...and she just wasn't ready for the battle she knew was coming.

The End

Books by Avery Gale

The Wolf Pack Series
Mated – Book One
Fated Magic – Book Two
Tempted by Darkness – Book Three

Masters of the Prairie Winds Club
Out of the Storm
Saving Grace
Jen's Journey
Bound Treasure
Punishing for Pleasure
Accidental Trifecta
Missionary Position

The ShadowDance Club
Katarina's Return – Book One
Jenna's Submission – Book Two
Rissa's Recovery – Book Three
Trace & Tori – Book Four
Reborn as Bree – Book Five
Red Clouds Dancing – Book Six
Perfect Picture – Book Seven

Club Isola

Capturing Callie – Book One

Healing Holly – Book Two

Claiming Abby – Book Three

I would love to hear from you!

Email:

avery.gale@ymail.com

Website:

www.averygalebooks.com/index.html

Facebook:

facebook.com/avery.gale.3

Instagram:

avery.gale

Twitter:

@avery_gale